HIGHLAND PASSAGE

HIGHLAND PASSAGE

A HIGHLAND PASSAGE NOVEL

J.L. JARVIS

BOOKBINDER PRESS

HIGHLAND PASSAGE
A Highland Passage Novel

Published by Bookbinder Press
bookbinderpress.com

ISBN: 978-0-9906476-0-7 (paperback)
ISBN: 978-0-9906476-1-4 (ebook)

PREFACE

I have often driven by the stone chambers of Putnam County, NY and wondered about them. While there is information available, much of it is conflicting. One theory is that they were built by ancient Celts. From that theory, my imagination took flight and *Highland Passage* was born.

- J.L. Jarvis

1

THE NOR'EASTER

"You're not trying hard enough," Cam hissed.

"I shouldn't have to try hard," answered Mac.

"Barton Hillman is perfectly suitable."

"For someone."

Cam narrowed her eyes.

"Look, either it's there or it isn't." Mac shrugged. "Tonight it wasn't."

"Or the time before this or the time before that. Do you realize how many times I've tried to find someone for you?"

"Do you realize how many times I've told you to stop?"

Frustration lined Cam's forehead. "I don't want you to be alone."

"I'm not. Every day I'm surrounded by people who love me."

"You're a kindergarten teacher." Cam rolled her eyes. "You know what I mean."

Mac glared at her sister. "But do you know what *I* mean? If I'm meant to be with someone, it will happen. If not, I'll be fine. Thank you. I love you. Now leave me alone." She grinned until Cam smiled back, and they hugged.

Hearing footsteps approach, Cam pulled the guests' coats from the closet. Cam's husband, in a well-rehearsed dance, helped Mac shrug into her coat. He leaned back just in time to avoid her sable tresses as she whipped them out from inside the collar. Cam handed a coat to their other guest, Barton.

While she slipped on her gloves, Mac watched the affable man layer one side of his cashmere scarf neatly over the other, matching the fringed ends precisely. As he buttoned his coat, Mac was tempted to give the scarf a tug just to make it askew. Resisting, she instead offered her hand and her most charming smile. "It was so nice to meet you, Martin."

"Barton." The corner of his mouth curved into an uncomfortable smile as he gave her gloved hand a cordial shake.

Mac winced as she felt a flush creep into her cheeks. "Barton. I'm so sorry."

Their hands slipped apart awkwardly. Barton offered a patient smile and then turned his attention to donning his own gloves. Barton Hillman was an executive at the same corporation where Mac's brother-in-law worked. He seemed smart enough. He was friendly, well bred, and impeccably groomed, as her sister had promised. Cam could have been describing a canine.

After planting a kiss on her brother-in-law's cheek, Mac said, "See you at Christmas."

"It's so early," Cam said. "Are you sure that you want to go now?"

Mac nodded. "Yes, I want to beat the weather." She peered at the sky, where the lightest flurry seemed to mock her. She fought back a frown as she willed the weather to support her excuse. The weatherman had predicted a wintery mix that would produce four to six inches of snow. Cam tossed her a wry glance, but Mac looked back unfazed. Lame as it was, she would own her excuse.

After the perfectly suitable Barton Hillman escorted her back to her car, Mac drove down the long, private road that led from her sister's affluent Westchester County home.

Mac's older sister had married her rich college boyfriend, according to plan. After losing their parents two years earlier in a car accident, Cam had set out with dogged determination to rebuild a life that was safe and secure. With both of her children in preschool, her life was in order, so she had turned to Mac's.

When she was only a few minutes from home, Mac pulled into a gas station off I-84. While waiting for the tank to fill, she watched the snow fall. The large flakes had begun nearly an hour earlier—just before she had started to cry—and had flown at her windshield and covered the ground in a thickening coating. That had really cut into a perfectly good cry. After an eye roll for Cam, who by setting her up tonight had reminded her yet again that she was single, Mac set thoughts of the evening aside. Sweats, fuzzy socks, and a good book were waiting for her by the fireplace. The best part was that it was only Friday. She had the rest of the weekend to enjoy being alone. All alone. Best part. Mac sighed.

After she was finished pumping, Mac slogged through the freezing slush to her car door and got in. She cursed as she fishtailed out of the station, and she proceeded more carefully down the highway.

"Okay," she said aloud. "Let's just get home safe-ly." A car passed with its brights on. "Thanks! No problem. I didn't need to see anyway." She tightened her grip on the wheel. "Sheesh, Mac, if you're going to be one of those single ladies who talk to themselves, you should at least get a cat so it'll look like you're talking to someone."

Pulling off the highway, she headed down the winding road to her home. Snow weighed down the branches of evergreen trees. Mac had to remind herself that such beauty could also be deadly. She had stood on her deck on such nights and looked into the woods as the cracking of ice-covered limbs cut through the stillness.

"Mind the road," she told herself as a tire caught a slick spot. Plows had not been through yet, and the snow was well over four inches and still falling.

Mac wondered how long ago it had started. The weather was always worse at her house than at her sister's. She regretted leaving Cam's until she remembered why she had made the decision. Cam had cornered her in the kitchen.

"Is that fictional man you're waiting for worth spending your life all alone?"

"I won't be alone. I'll have you." Mac grinned.

Cam did not. "But you need your own life."

Those were the words that had cut her. They had always been a team, named Cameron and Mackenzie after their mother's Scottish ancestors. Love for their ancestral home had been passed down through the generations. Their great-grandfather had told his children, and they in turn told theirs, that in each generation, one child would long for the homeland. Mac had always known she was the one, and Cam had always made fun of her for being born in the wrong place and time.

MAC HAD ONCE MADE the mistake of leaving her book on a table when her sister came over. The cover showed a muscular hunk wearing nothing but a kilt and clutching a small-waisted woman while the wind blew his hair and left hers untouched.

With a derisive wave toward the book, Cam had said, "Is that what you want for a husband?"

Mac dismissed her with a smirk. "Of course not! He can be wearing a shirt."

Cam rolled her eyes and exhaled, but she also gave up. Score one for Mac.

Mac smiled at the memory but grew somber when she recalled what else Cam had said in the kitchen that night.

"You can't live life alone."

"And why not?" Mac asked.

"You'll be lonely."

"Not as lonely as I'd be if I married without love."

Cam's face showed no inkling of understanding.

Mac continued, "I don't know where to find it—or if I ever will. If I can't, then I'll live alone; if I can, then I'll know it was meant to be."

Cam shook her head. "It's not like in the novels."

For you. Mac bit back those words. "Maybe not. But I know what I want."

"And what's that?"

"I want someone whose arms feel like home."

"And how will you ever know, when you won't let a man within arm's length?"

———

MAC'S EYES misted with tears. She feared her sister was right. Even so, she would rather live alone than with Martin—Barton. He was nice, but if she had wanted to live with someone nice, she'd go back to college and get a roommate. She didn't want a roommate; she wanted a soul mate. That was the part that made Cam smirk. Well, Cam could do what she wanted. She'd made the life that she wanted, and she was happy.

"And I'm doing what I want," Mac said to herself. *Going home to my empty house.*

She drove past an old stone chamber, one of dozens scattered about Putnam County, New York. The stacked stone structures were too small to be dwellings. They were more like manmade caves that had been weathered and overgrown with grass and moss until they blended into the landscape. Many of them lay deep in the woods; others sat like lonely relics beside country roads. Some thought the ancient Celts had built them, but no one knew for sure.

Up ahead, moonlight gave the chamber a magical glow. Beside it, something moved. Deer?

"No, they're too smart to be out in weather like this, unlike me."

Mac's headlights lit up a man clad in a kilt and black doublet. He stepped onto the road and held his arms up to signal her to stop.

"What the hell?" Mac said.

She slammed her foot on the brake pedal and went into a skid that spun her. The car moved too fast and bounced too much for her to see which way to steer—not that steering would change anything. With a bang, she stopped, and the airbag deployed. She had run into the side of the mountain. That would have alarmed her if the acrid smell from the airbag had not overpowered her senses. She waved her hands, trying to clear the cloud of dust, while "Sleigh Ride" played on the stereo and her horn blared from the impact. She turned the stereo off and leaned her head back against the headrest to steady her breathing and her pounding heart.

Through the steam rising out of her car, she spied a large tree that had fallen across the road. If the kilted man had not stepped into the road to stop her, she would have plowed head-on into the tree. Kilted man? Mac looked about. He was gone.

"Great. I'm hallucinating. That car horn is real, though." She needed to get out of the car. She struggled to get the keys out of the ignition, but they wouldn't budge. The car was still in drive but was crunched into a boulder that jutted out into the road. After a struggle with the gearshift, she got it into park and pulled out her keys. Her horn didn't stop. Dizzying frustration roiled within her. "I can't think with that noise."

Her head swam. She pulled the door handle, but it was stuck. She had to get out of the car. She leaned her throbbing head back on the headrest and turned toward the passenger side. It was too close to the rocks. She would have to ease her way out through the driver's side window. Mac's hand trembled as she unbuckled her seat belt. Her vision blurred and began to go dark. *Don't faint now.*

The door creaked and then opened. A deep male voice said, "Come, lass." Strong arms pulled her from the car. "Can you stand?"

He set her on her feet, but her legs buckled. He scooped her up. Fuzzyheaded, Mac leaned on his chest. Her hand rested on his shoulder, and her fingers traced a fold of wool draped over his doublet.

"Nice kilt, Scotty. But just so you know, real Scotsmen go shirtless." She smiled and laid her head on his shoulder.

2

THIS MOMENT

MAC AWOKE to the smell of wood smoke and the feel of strong arms holding her. She tried to sit up, but the arms tightened.

In low, calming tones, the Scotsman said, "You're safe. I'll not harm you."

"Not harm me?" That brought her fully alert. "Why would you even say that? Who are you? Where are we?" She winced as pain shot through her temple.

"You've bumped your head."

"With what, a ten-pound hammer?" She tenderly touched her head to assess the damage.

Fire lit the rough ceiling and walls of what looked like a cave—a cave barely large enough for the two of them. She was nestled in the man's lap. Mac's situation did not look good. She was trapped in a cave with a large, rugged man. How she got there, she couldn't recall. He'd probably clubbed her over the head and dragged her there by her hair. But where was there? Past the fire, rough-hewn stones framed the falling snow.

"The stone chamber," she whispered.

"I beg your pardon, lass?"

Lass? And with a Scottish burr? That was cute.

Mac turned to look at him but quickly turned back, refusing to be drawn in by his looks. Dim firelight or not, she knew handsome when she saw it. Tousled brown hair brushed his temples. Those eyes were dark and warm, and they'd searched hers a little too deeply. She had to work hard to resist him. Her practical side was, thank God, stronger.

"I'm a black belt," she warned. "If you try anything, I can kill you." She prayed he wouldn't ask her what she had a black belt in. She had one—in her belt drawer. It came with her little black dress.

He laughed at her threat, and his laugh was full and infectious. She forced a stern look to hide the urge to laugh with him.

"I'll be careful not to anger you then." Even his smirk was good-looking.

Mac nodded. "See that you don't."

He answered her nod with his own while suppressing a grin. With that settled, she became aware of his body against hers. Her inner sirens sounded. With a jab of her elbows into his chest, she pushed up, grabbing his thighs for leverage. She lifted a brow. *Don't let those rock-hard muscles distract you. Keep moving.*

He leaned back, raising his palms in surrender. "Dinnae *fash yersel*, lass. I was trying to warm you. You were shaking before you awoke."

"I'm not *fashing* myself—whatever that is. But if I feel like *fashing*, I'll *fash* as much as I want." *Fashing* or not, she felt cold away from his arms. She wouldn't think about that. "I would like an explanation, if that's not too much to ask."

"An explanation of what?"

"Of why we're here, for starters."

"I pulled you from your carriage and brought you here for shelter and warmth."

She glared at him in disbelief.

"Here you are, sheltered and warmed. I've not hurt you, have I?"

"Maybe you were waiting for me to wake up." She eyed him with more mistrust than she felt, but she wouldn't let him know how strangely unthreatening he seemed. Sick bastards counted on trust to lure victims. Of course, he had no need to lure, since she was already in his lair. They were inside a shelter too far from houses for anyone to hear if she screamed, which was all the more reason not to trust him. He might be some perv who'd wandered off the Appalachian Trail. It ran past her house, which, unfortunately, was still too far of a walk in this storm. "Are you a hiker?"

"Nay, lass."

The soft light in his eyes and his quiet confidence unsettled her more than she dared to let on. He met every skeptical look, every challenging edge in her voice with a calm hint of a smile.

She turned away, afraid the firelight might reveal the color he brought to her cheeks. He had clouded her thinking, so she latched onto the last thing he had said. "What's with the lass stuff, anyway?"

He looked quizzically at her.

"The way you're talking. You're good, but I've been to Scotland. That accent's fake."

That seemed to amuse him. "Is it, now?"

She scrutinized him. "Where have I seen you before?"

"In front of your carriage."

"My carriage? Oh, you mean my car. Yeah, I guess that's it." Their eyes met and lingered too long. She glanced down to avoid the power of his gaze. "What's up with that kilt? Are you in a pipe band?"

"It's a plaid."

She opened her mouth to protest, but he was right. She shrugged. "Sorry, plaid. Who are you? Do you live around here?" The houses in her area were so far apart that a person could go months without seeing a neighbor. Perhaps that was how she knew him.

"Nay."

Without even looking at him, she felt his guileless gaze. It enlivened her nerves, which was reason enough to beware. Overwhelmed by the strength of his presence, she couldn't come up with her usual quips that put most guys off. She felt lost. She didn't like that sensation.

"Why do I feel like I should know you?" she asked.

"Do you?"

Something in his searching look made her want to say yes. She puzzled over it then exhaled and shook her head. "That bump on the head did a number on me."

He nodded and stared into the darkness—but not before Mac saw his disappointment. She found herself wishing she hadn't been the cause. A gust blew in some snow, and Mac shivered. In one motion, he slipped the end of his plaid over her shoulders. She stiffened and turned to defend herself, but his stern look cautioned her not to.

"Are you going to hurt me?" she asked.

"Hurt you?" He looked annoyed. "Lass, do you not think I'd have done it by now if I wanted to?" His anger faded as he saw the fear in her eyes. "*Och*, you wee fool. I told you that I wouldnae harm you, but I will keep you warm if you'll let me." He looked at her, his outstretched arms suspended between embrace and retreat. With a nod, he lowered his arms. "Aye, well, I'll not put you in fear. I'll stay over here by the wall. Warm yourself by the fire. I give you my word, I'll not trouble you."

She eyed him as he put distance between them. She drew farther away, as close to the fire as she could get without snow falling on her. She needed to make her way home. He might fall asleep, and she could steal away into the darkness. With any luck, the snow would keep up long enough to cover her tracks. Her house wasn't far down the road. If she could make it there, she could call someone for help.

But what would she tell anyone she might call? *A stranger pulled me from a wreck and warmed me by the fire, where he proceeded not to lay a hand on me?* There must be a local ordinance against unsolicited gentlemanliness. Yeah… and those long, powerful legs ought to be outlawed. She'd had quite a good look at them. Under normal circumstances, she'd be wary of him for far different reasons. Men like him drew attention from everyone. Who would want a lifetime of being judged unworthy beside someone as good-looking as him?

Whoa, Mac. You're supposed to be planning your escape, not your marriage!

She glanced at him. True to his word, he hadn't moved; he wasn't even looking at her. The firelight caught his profile as he stared into the night. She studied him further. Hair dark as coffee, full lips— probably soft and warm. *Good grief, Mac. Get a grip.*

As though hearing her, he turned and made eye contact. "'Tis wise for you to be cautious. You dinnae ken me, so you've no reason to trust me. But I wish you'd not fear me. I've done naught to harm you."

She hugged her knees. "So far."

"Mac? Do you not ken me?" His expression was tinged with frustration. "I mean know."

"I know what ken means." His gaze troubled her. Unbidden sorrow haunted his eyes. Her heart ached as she whispered, "Please stop."

He shook his head slightly. She might not have seen it had he not turned to the fire with his clenched jaw.

Mac said, "Don't look at me like that."

He let out his breath and gave a casual shake of his head. "I'm sorry. The firelight must have played tricks with my eyes. For a moment, you looked like someone I once knew." He smiled, but it was forced.

"Did she hurt you?"

"Hurt me? *Och*, no."

"I'm sorry, I thought—"

"She would never have hurt me." He stared at the snow.

"You loved her?"

"I love her still. I've risked everything to find her."

"Oh. The way you talked, I thought she might have died."

"Perhaps she did, in a way." He glanced at her. "We were parted and lost one another."

Mac nodded. A pang of longing took her by surprise. Such emotions could only distract her, along with the little things she was noticing—his strong jawline stubbled with a day's growth of beard and those lips. Her eyes kept coming back to those lips. He turned toward her, and she lifted her eyes to meet his knowing look. He had noticed her studying him, and he did not object.

Doing her best to look neutral, Mac said, "So she lives around here?"

"Aye." He hesitated, as though trying to form just the right words. "We met not far from here."

"Oh?"

He looked away. "It has been a long time. I was daft to think we would be as we were."

"So you've seen her already?"

"Aye." He stared into the flames and smiled to himself. "It was not the right time. And what of you?"

She frowned. "Me?"

"Is there a man?"

She didn't like that question and made a sharp turn to miss it. "I'm with a man right now—a very strange man." She grinned.

He grinned in return. "Aye, a strange man who found you shelter and then made a fire to warm you."

"Thank you, but—stop me if I'm wrong—you'd have done that anyway for yourself. So if you're thinking I owe you anything, I don't."

He let out a full-throated laugh. "You misunderstand me, my lady."

"Really? Like a little 'my lady' will make it all better. You Brits think we all get stupid over an accent—"

His eyes blazed. "Madam, I am a Scot."

"Well, Scotty, last I looked, Scotland was part of the UK."

His face went ashen. "The what?"

"The United Kingdom. Hey, are you okay?" *Other than being unhinged…*

He looked away and suppressed whatever shock he felt. "Oh, aye. I am well." He returned his focus to her. "But you're shivering. Come here, lass." He opened his arms and beckoned her to him.

Mac eyed him. His expression was open and honest. She found herself trusting him for no reason other than her gut feeling. Despite his sturdy physique, he was gentle. It was in his eyes. They were large and deeply set, looking at the world with guileless kindness and sympathy—perhaps even sadness. Once more, her gaze fell to his mouth. Her eyes darted away as she tried to think clearly. He stretched out his hand.

She had doubts, but she placed her hand in his and let him draw her closer. Despite her pounding heart, she assured him, "I'm just in it for the warmth. Don't get any ideas."

"Dinnae *fash yersel* over me."

Mac's face wrinkled. "I give up. What does *fash* mean?"

Suppressing a grin, he said, "Dinnae trouble yourself, my lady."

My lady? Damn, he had charm. The sort of charm serial killers must have to lure their victims into the dark and stormy woods. She glanced at him, and his admiring look made her feel stupid, a fact she did her best to conceal. Her best wasn't good enough. She exhaled a little too loudly.

"Why do you sigh, lass?" They'd drawn close—for the warmth—so he needed only to tilt his head down to peer at her.

His warm breath brushed her cheek, and she shivered. "I, uh, oh, I'm just sighing from the cold. Whew! It's cold!" She made a great show of rubbing her arms.

Outside, thick flakes drifted noiselessly to the ground. A person could die out there without anyone knowing; the body might not be found until the spring thaw. The Scotsman's arm tightened around Mac, and he pulled her against his broad shoulders and chest. The man was a furnace.

"How is it you're not freezing your…whatever off in that kilt? Sorry, plaid. From what I hear—never mind." She had heard that they wore nothing underneath.

"Might I ask you a question?"

She looked up with a start.

"To distract us, you ken, from the cold." His mouth spread into a boyish grin that lit his face.

If he was a creep, he wasn't a very good one. She hadn't felt such ease with a man since… well, ever. For all the dates her sister had arranged for her, none of those men had looked at her and seen her—or made her feel—the way this man did. He was—something she couldn't even think.

"What are you thinking?" he asked.

Her posture stiffened as she shrugged.

"You were shaking your head."

She averted her eyes. "I'm shaking. It's freezing."

"*Och*, 'tis not so bad." He grinned. "We're inside."

She looked at the stones that surrounded them. "I suppose you could call it that."

"Aye, and we've a fire to warm us."

As he repositioned his arms, Mac gave in and leaned into his embrace. She was cold—cold enough to reconsider her options. "Look—" She lifted her chin and peered at him. "What's your name?"

"Ciarán."

"I'm—"

"Mackenzie."

Slowly, she nodded. "But most people call me—"

"Mac."

She flashed him a suspicious look. "Yeah."

His eyes sharpened as he looked outside. "When I pulled you from your carriage—your car—a bag fell out."

"Oh, my purse."

His face relaxed.

"Where is it?" she asked.

He pulled it from the shadows and handed it to her.

She rummaged through the leather bag and pulled out her phone. "There's horrible coverage around here, but we could get lucky." After she pressed the screen a few times, she held it to her ear and looked out at the falling snow, waiting. Then she tried texting. "Nothing. Why would I get lucky tonight?" Mac turned to assess her companion. "I live down the road. I think we could hike through this snow in an hour."

"Are you sure?"

"I'm sure that I'm freezing my butt off. In an hour, we could be inside by a fire with some blankets and whisky to warm us."

He eyed her three-inch heels. "You'll not get far in those."

She gave him a frank look. "I'm motivated."

"Hand me your slippers."

Mac's brow creased. "Why?"

Without a word, he held out his hand. She slipped them off and handed them to him. He hit them against the rocks and pried the heels off with his dirk. Then he ripped two strips from his plaid and tied her shoes onto her feet, crisscrossing the plaid around her calf and tying off the ends. After dousing the fire, Ciarán offered his hand to Mac. Then off they went.

With careful steps, Mac moved through the snow, trying not to show how biting the cold was on her legs and feet. The ground was uneven beneath the snow, testing her balance and strength. Her feet grew numb.

After several laborious steps, Ciarán said, "My lady—"

"I am not your lady."

"Mistress—"

"I'm nobody's mistress."

After a low, exasperated sigh, he said, "Lass."

Did he have to say that? She had read enough Scottish romance novels to go weak in the knees at the sound, which was something she couldn't afford at the moment. She kept up her slow tramping.

"I cannae let you go further. Your legs will stiffen soon, if they haven't already. You'll get stuck, and your skin will turn black—if the bears dinnae get to you first."

She stopped. Bears? There had been a few sightings… "Oh, good try. They're hibernating." She felt satisfied with herself until she looked around. There was only a sliver of moonlight. She could barely make out the road. If she took a wrong turn, they could become lost. The house lights could have guided them, but there were none on right now. "The power must be out."

"Lass?"

"The power. There's no light."

He cautiously said, "Well, 'tis night."

Mac squinted at him. Was he joking? Mac turned and looked into the darkness and then looked in the opposite direction. "Okay, I give up. Where's the road?"

"This way." He took her elbow to help her. "Are you sure you can do this?"

She shrugged carelessly. "Sure, why not? I'm fine." A few steps later, her foot landed in a rut, and Mac fell.

Ciarán caught her and heaved her up over his shoulder.

"Wait! What are you doing?" she asked as he turned back toward the stone chamber.

Without missing a step, Ciarán said, "I'm keeping you safe."

"But I want to go home."

"Aye, well, staying alive will have to do for the now." His brawny legs made quick work of the rest of the hill. He set her down at the stone chamber's entrance.

She brushed snow-dampened hair from her eyes. "Well. Here we are. Would you like to come in for some coffee?" She laughed. "Just kidding."

He looked at her blankly and then led her back into the stone chamber. Mac shivered, unable to stop.

"I'll light the fire." He crouched and pulled a tinderbox from his sporran.

She had slept through the previous fire-lighting procedure, so she watched with interest. "Who lights a fire like that anymore? I know you said you're from Scotland, but what century?"

"Eighteenth."

Mac looked for a sign that he was joking. "Yeah, right."

Mac watched the fire-making process with wonder. He smiled at her, but a hint of sorrow seemed to linger behind it. Now that the fire was started, the Scotsman rose and unwrapped the plaid from his shoulder and waist.

"Hold on there, Rob Roy. Keep your plaid on." She held her palm out with as threatening a look as she could muster.

He stepped back and raised his palms, still holding

the fabric between thumb and forefinger. "If you share this with me, we might both stay warm through the night."

"I wish I had a dollar for every guy who's said that."

He made no effort to hide his smile. His gaze swept from her hair to her lips, and his face shone with amusement.

"What?" she said defensively. His gaze lingered until she blushed. "You don't believe me? It could happen."

His eyes rested on hers with a soft look that warmed her, though she wouldn't admit it. "Lass—"

"Call me Mac."

"Very well. Mac, will you share the plaid with me? It's very warm."

Mac was cold enough to do anything to stay warm. She nodded and let him wrap the plaid around her. Her teeth chattered, and he held her.

When she warmed up enough to talk, she smoothed her fingertips over the leather that covered his chest. "Nice jacket."

"My doublet?"

She grinned and lifted her eyes. "Come on, fess up. Did Cam send you over as a joke?"

"Cam?"

"Because I read Scottish romance books. I get it. Tell her I laughed out loud. Ha." When he looked at her strangely, she smirked. "Are you some sort of singing telegram, only without the song? Oh, you're not one of those—y'know—stripper telegrams, are you?" She glanced at him and then averted her gaze. "Cam's gone too far."

"I dinnae ken what you mean."

She studied him, unsure whether to believe him. She shook her head. "Never mind." She stared into the fire. Mesmerized by the flickering flames, Mac yawned.

The Scotsman guided her head to his shoulder. "Try to sleep." His warm breath gave her a chill, but not the cold kind.

Mac nodded. She didn't need convincing. "I would like to know one thing, though."

"And what would that be?" His voice sounded amused.

"Who are you?"

"I've told you my name."

"Ciarán what?"

"MacRae." He rested his cheek on the top of her head.

"Ciarán MacRae," she said softly. "I can't figure you out."

"You can sleep on it, lass." He brushed his lips over her hair, and then she closed her eyes.

BRIGHT SUN SHONE into the stone chamber's entrance. Mac awoke next to Ciarán, warmed by his body. On her arm lay his large hand, rough and well-shaped. She felt safe and at home in his arms. The feeling was foreign, and she didn't trust it. He stirred and repositioned his arms around her. The plaid was coarse and uneven, as if woven by hand. Mac touched the fabric. Not even Cam would have gone to such trouble.

In response to her touch, he planted a drowsy kiss on her forehead and drifted back to sleep. Mac gasped, shut her eyes, and exhaled. She should wake him, but his breath was so warm on her neck. She wasn't quite ready to lose the sense of belonging she felt in his arms. That in itself was good reason to leave. She was experiencing some sort of Stockholm syndrome—not that she'd fallen in love! Nor was she held captive. She could leave. It was light out. She could find her way home without him, and she would. Mac eased Ciarán's hand aside, taking care not to wake him. She was about to slip out of his arms when he murmured something and cupped his hand on her breast.

Mac scrambled to her feet. "Now you're in trouble."

Ciarán rose abruptly and looked outside for signs of danger. Seeing none, he took hold of her shoulders. "Are you all right, Mac? *Och*, 'tis not a proper name for a woman so fair." His words trailed off as he gazed into her eyes.

She should have said something glib to put distance between them, but she just stared, slack-jawed. Too many moments later, she forced her gaze away. "Don't flatter me, Ciarán. It won't work." If she said it enough, she might believe it.

"No, I ken that you wouldnae countenance flattery. 'Tis why I spoke only the truth."

God, he's good. She turned back to him, ready to toss out her best sarcastic quip, but his unguarded gaze disarmed her. She lost herself in it, unable to speak. Ciarán smiled an admiring, trustworthy smile. She almost believed it.

Mac turned and kicked snow onto the fire's glowing embers. "I've got to go."

Ciarán wrapped and belted his plaid then joined her outside the stone chamber. He squinted as the bright snow reflected the sunlight. "Would you leave me here then, to fend for myself?"

"Oh, I'm sure you can manage without me." Mac turned to find Ciarán inside her personal space. Her voice lost its self-assured tone as she looked at him. She lost track of her purpose when his full lips parted. Unsettled, she drew back, but he touched her chin. She began to protest, but his gaze was so tender that her breath caught.

"Mac." He made no move to kiss her, but his soft gaze fell to her lips.

She found her eyes drifting to his mouth as well. The kiss was there, waiting for her. "No." She had built a life. She controlled it. Who was he to disrupt it? She turned away and stared at the brilliant snow and the stark winter trees.

He rested his hands on her shoulders. "I must leave you soon. May I kiss you good-bye?"

Her cautious look was his answer.

"Can you not trust me by now?"

Fear would not drown out the drumming of her heart. Tears stung her eyes. How dare he... How could he affect her so? "You're a stranger."

With a pained nod, he said, "Aye, that I am." He searched the sky and exhaled. "If there were but words to tell you—"

"Please don't." She was surprised by the chill in her voice. Was Cam right? Had Mac become so adept at keeping men distant that she didn't know how to let one get close?

Quiet and sure, he closed the distance between them. "You've spent the night in my arms."

"For the warmth."

"You ken as well as I do that there was more."

She did, but she wouldn't admit it. She shook her head but stopped when the tip of his finger traced her lips. Against her will, her lips parted. She grasped his hand. Even the scratches and scars on his hand were appealing. Why couldn't she breathe?

He drew her palm to his lips. "Mac, I ken that you dinnae remember me."

She was breathless but managed to shake her head. "Oh, I think I'd remember you."

His eyes shone with a hint of a smile, but it faded. He placed Mac's hand on his chest. "Do you feel that?"

She nodded, feeling the strong beat against her palm.

"That is my heart, and it's yours."

She stared at his chest. "Please." *Stop.* She couldn't voice that word.

"How can I win your trust?"

Scarcely a whisper came out. "Give me time."

He lifted her chin. "*Och*, lass, I dinnae have that to give."

"It's too much, too fast—"

"Aye, I ken it." His expression softened.

"But you can't—because I don't understand it myself."

He brushed a tear that had slid to her cheek. He frowned at the sunrise. "There is no more time for us now." Snow caught sparks of sunlight around them. Gripping her shoulders, he took in the sight of her hair, cheekbones, and mouth. "I must leave."

She couldn't let him go without knowing his kiss,

how it tasted and felt. So with a gasp, she lifted her face and kissed him. Souls could join with a kiss, but the hearts that housed them would break the next instant.

With a groan, he spoke against her lips. "It is not our time now, but I'll come back for you, Mac." He smiled at her name. "Lovely Mac, I will love you, and you will love me." He glanced at the bright sun shining into the stone chamber. "*Och*, 'tis time."

Mac opened her mouth to ask what he meant, but he stole one more kiss.

"Remember this moment. I promise you more." He turned and walked into the stone chamber.

Mac put her hand on the stone entryway to steady herself. She felt dizzy and weak. "Ciarán, where are you going?"

He turned to look back and smiled. "I'm a traveler, lass. I cannae stay here."

"I don't understand."

"You'll think me daft if I tell you, but you'll ken when I'm gone."

"No, I think you're daft now." She smiled, but tears blurred her vision.

"I live in the past."

"Me too. That's what Cam always tells me, but—"

"Mac, listen to me." With a flinch, he pulled back. "'Tis too late." He held his palm up to caution her to stay back.

Ignoring his warning, Mac rushed toward him and held his hand. A shock traveled through her. She pulled back her hand.

"Dinnae touch me again."

"But why?" She rubbed her wrist, which was tingling and numb.

He smiled sadly. "Will you wait for me?"

"Yes, if you kiss me like that again." Mac's lips spread into a smile that would not be repressed.

"You're the one who kissed me."

The last thing she saw was his smile. Blinding light shone from the sun behind her and from inside the chamber, like two mirrors reflecting each other. The brilliant light washed over Ciarán.

And he disappeared.

She could still hear him saying, "Lovely Mac, I will love you, and you will love me." The last part of his promise was already true. He was gone, and she may have gone mad. But she knew he would come back. Until then, she would remember that moment.

3

THE STONE CHAMBER

NOT EVERYONE BELIEVES in love at first sight. Mackenzie Cooper was one of those people. It had taken her more than six hours to fall in love with a Highland time traveler. Even now, she felt like a fool, first for letting herself love and then worse—for letting herself hope. There was no logical way to explain what had happened, so she did not try. That much she had accepted. And love—well, that could be explained away, too. What she had felt was a chemical reaction. The guy was hot. Just the right length of hair, a rich medium brown, barely touching his shoulders; and eyes—who could argue with blue? Not a deep shade of blue, but a silvery blue that shone when he looked at her. That was the thing. When he looked in her eyes with that shimmering warmth, her heart did all those things that hearts do just before bodies take over. But what got to her most was the way he was with her. He was honest. After years of erecting defenses, Mac trusted him.

Mac told no one about that night. As the weeks and months turned into a year, she could not forget. She had seen a man travel through time, and that man had made her a promise. He would love her, and she would love him. But Mac feared they might never find one another again.

For more than a year, she went every day to the place where she had met him. The stone chamber was just down the road from her house. If pressed, she could not explain why she went back. Somewhere along the way, Mac had given up hope that she might ever see him again, but she continued to go as one might visit a grave to pay one's respects, reconciled to the sadness of loss giving way to the bittersweet comfort of memories. She went because she could no more help it than she could help the heartache that sprang from the thought of him. In those few hours together, Ciarán MacRae had found his way into her soul, and she would not forget him. As much peace as she knew anymore, she found here, sitting alone by the chamber. So, for now, the warm sun and the scent of the grass were her solace.

A soft mist fell as trees whispered of rain, and the scent of the earth and damp stones rose up and hung in the air. Lifting her face to the sky, Mac breathed it all in as the cool mist soothed her face. But dark clouds rolled in overhead. If she left now, she might make it home merely damp before the sky opened with rain. David rode past on his bike, unaware that she was there. She sighed and then felt guilty for being relieved that he had not seen her. She wanted just a few more moments alone with her memories of Ciarán.

David Kowalski taught fifth-grade science at the school where Mac worked. He was also her friend. At times Mac wondered if he might wish for more, but they had never broached the subject of feelings. He used to stop by her house for coffee on Saturday mornings, but he had not been by in some time.

Shadows of thickening clouds draped themselves over the trees as Mac gathered her bag and water bottle. Sunlight peeked through a small gap in the clouds and shone into the stone chamber, but Mac didn't notice as she briskly brushed the dirt from her jeans. Once finished, she indulged in one last gaze into the stone chamber, where a faint light now broke through. The back wall faded like a morning mist and lifted to reveal the same scene she had seen behind Ciarán when he disappeared. From the clearing mist, a man appeared, facing the opposite direction of her. He wore plaid.

"Ciarán!" Mac called and stepped closer. He turned. For a moment they stared, with the same stunned expression. He walked through the mist toward her until it was clear that it was not Ciarán at all. His hair was lighter but darkened by rain, and uneven stubble dappled his leathery face. He reached out, gripped her arm tightly, and pulled her inside. Mac fought him, but he was ruggedly built, with a feral smell of earth, body, and blood that assaulted her senses.

He gave her arm a painful yank, jarring a clump of hair free from its clip. By reflex, she reached up and caught hold of her hair clip. With all the force she could muster, she jabbed it in his face. He cried out a curse but held onto her with one arm and yanked her closer. A shiver of an electrical current passed through her to him, and he shuddered. Unable to pull herself free, Mac leaned the full weight of her body away from her attacker. In doing so, her foot slipped on the loose stones. She stumbled, and the force of her fall pulled her free. She reached out to break her fall and barely missed a small rock on the ground. She grabbed hold of the rock and started to scramble toward the mouth of the chamber, but a hand clamped around her ankle.

Mac screamed and rolled over, jabbing her boot heel at his groin, squarely striking her target. Her attacker paused in his tracks, long enough for Mac to land another strong kick that threw him off-balance so that he staggered back into the stone wall behind him.

Except he did not fall against it. He dissolved and went through it.

Mac lay stunned for a moment. Fearing that he might return, she pulled herself up and ran out of the stone chamber and back to her house. She drew near the porch steps and flinched at the sound of a voice.

"Out running already? Well, aren't you the early bird?"

"David?" she panted, her heart still pounding with lingering fear.

David rested comfortably in an old wooden porch chair. "The sun's barely up." He rose long enough to pull a coffee from the cup holder clamped to his bicycle handlebars. When he first got it, they had laughed about the extra geek factor it gave him; all he needed to complete the picture was some plastic streamers on his handlebars.

Mac was not laughing now at the image. With a furtive glance back toward the stone chamber, she took the coffee and thanked him.

"What happened to you?" He stared at her forearm, which was already showing signs of emerging bruises.

Mac looked at her arm and tried to shrug it off, but it was hard to ignore. "It must've happened when I fell earlier."

"You fell? How?" He examined her arm, looking doubtful.

Mac shrugged again. "Running."

"In the woods? You weren't on the road; I came from the same direction."

Mac glanced around. "Yeah, I like nature. So what's in the bag?"

David pulled a bagel from the small paper bag in his hand and offered it to her.

"No, thanks. I'm not hungry."

"Not hungry?" David chuckled. "I don't know what that is." He was baiting her now; he knew how she hated the way he could eat all he wanted and not gain an ounce. He grinned, expecting a reaction.

Mac tried to smile back, but her stomach was churning. A ferocious Highlander had just attacked her. Her heart had not yet stopped hammering in her rib cage. No, she was not hungry.

"Here, you can save it for later." He took a bite of his bagel and offered the bag to her. "There's another for you in the bag."

Mac set the bag down on the porch rail and then sipped the warm coffee while awkward silence hovered between them.

"David, why are you here?" She had not meant to be blunt, but she was too shaken for small talk.

"I was in the neighborhood."

"David, no one's just in the neighborhood here. I live in the woods on the side of a mountain."

He smiled. "Busted. I was worried about you."

"Worried? Why?"

"I don't know. Lately, you've seemed a bit off."

"Off?" If "off" meant gone mad—well, then yes, she was a bit off. She had lost the only man she might ever have loved, and mere minutes ago, she had fought off a feral time traveler who had leapt out of the chamber and sent him packing. Her heart sank as she realized that, in her frantic need to escape her attacker, she had missed a chance to pass through the chamber to Ciarán's time. She must have gasped in dismay, for David was eyeing her with alarm.

"Mac?" He touched her shoulder. When she flinched, he let go immediately.

Mac's attention shifted down the road to the sunlight that now brightened the trees on its way to the stone chamber. "Look, David. I'm sorry, but I've got to go." She thrust the coffee cup at him and turned, leaving him standing agape, coffee in hand, as she trudged down the road toward the stone chamber.

"Mac?" Met with silence, he called out again and followed her. "Got to go where? Got a date with a fox?" He laughed at himself.

Without turning, Mac said, "Sorry. I can't explain now."

Several minutes later, she reached the chamber. She went inside and turned back toward the sunlight. David caught up to her at the entrance.

She swatted at him. "Move, David. You're blocking the sun."

"What?"

"Just wait out there." When he failed to move, Mac added, "Please?"

He thought she was nuts. It was all over his face. But he did as she asked and moved out of sight, to the side of the entrance. Mac stood inside the stone chamber, facing out toward the sun, and waited. She glanced over her shoulder but saw only stone. Still, she waited. The warmth of the sun washed her face in light. David peeked around the corner, but she gave him her stern teacher face, and he pivoted back. She shut her eyes and tried to remember what Ciarán had done before he vanished. But he had not done anything except stand there. He had held his palm out to stop her, and something electric happened. He had not been surprised. He had known it was coming. Clearly he had done it before. She remembered the sensation—like an electrical tingle. She felt none of it now, and the light gave way to thick clouds.

David flinched as she emerged from the chamber. "C'mon, let's go warm up that coffee."

Ignoring his wrinkled brow, Mac started back toward the road.

Minutes later, they were at her kitchen table, hot coffee in hand. David leaned his lanky frame back and propped his feet up on the chair beside him. "So, Mac, do you want to tell me what that was about?"

"No." She got up to refill the small pitcher of cream even though it did not need refilling.

David quietly watched her. As Mac sank back down into her chair, he said, "I may just be a science nerd, but I see what you're doing."

"Avoiding your questions?" She looked at him frankly. It took effort to seem this nonchalant.

David nodded. "Yeah, pretty much."

Mac flashed a smile that did not reach her eyes. "Well, good. So that's settled."

"Not quite. About the stone chamber…"

"What about it? It's stone. It's a chamber." Her glib attitude only made her appear less at ease.

"But you went inside it."

"I did."

"Why?"

"Because it was there and I felt like it."

Unconvinced, David stared at her and folded his arms. A long and uncomfortable silence followed.

Mac heaved a sigh. "Look, David, there was a reason, but I'm not going to discuss it. Okay?"

He searched her eyes. To her credit, she met his gaze directly.

"Okay. Fair enough. But I'm worried about you." He grew quiet as he watched her slowly circle a spoon through her coffee. "Your hands are trembling."

She let go of the spoon so that it clinked against the cup and reflexively clutched her hands in her lap.

David continued, "Mac, something's wrong. I don't want to pry. I just want to be a friend and help you if I can."

She could not let him see how his concern not only moved her but also made her want to confide in him. She was bursting to talk to someone about her bizarre experiences, which was exactly what she could not do. It would just make things worse. Not only would he not believe her, but he would think that she'd lost it. No, she could not tell him, now or ever.

"David, you are my friend. And you're right. There is something, but it's nothing to worry about. Really." She leaned forward, elbows on the table, looking at him conspiratorially. "I've met someone." She shrugged and offered a guilty smile.

"So you've met someone. Good. And because of this someone, you had to rush over to the stone chamber to…what?"

Her eyes widened. To avoid his uncomfortable gaze, Mac went for the coffee pot and refilled his cup, giving her time to think.

"Meditate."

David grimaced. "I'm sorry. Let me get this straight. You've met someone, so while we were talking, you had to make a quick dash down the road to meditate."

Mac tried to act as though this made perfect sense. "Yes. He—my man—suggested I meditate. I told him how stressful it is working with children, so he told me to try it." She exhaled, feeling pleased with herself.

"In the stone chamber?"

Mac nodded, now committed to her story, no matter how lame it might sound. And it did. But she soldiered on. "Sensory deprivation." She lifted her brows and gave a knowing nod. "Makes it easier to focus."

Now slack-jawed, David stared in disbelief for a moment and then relaxed. "I get it. You know, you could have just told me you don't want to talk."

"No, that's not what I meant." She wanted to reassure him, but how? Nothing about it made sense. "Look, I'm fine. And I think it's very sweet of you to worry about me."

"Yeah, sweet. I get that a lot."

His smirk made Mac smile. "Aw, David. You're such a good friend."

He nodded. "Just don't punch my shoulder and tell me what a great pal I am. Oh, wait, you practically did that already."

Mac grinned. "I promise not to punch you." She gave him a pat on the arm and then stood up.

Seeing his cue, David rose and moved toward the door. "If you need anything—"

"I'll text you. But I won't need to, because I'm fine." Her warm smile was almost convincing.

David paused in the doorway for one last probing gaze before he gave up with a sigh and turned toward the door. "You know how to reach me if you need to."

"I do. Thank you, David," she called out as he got on his bike.

After he had gone from sight, Mac let out the breath she had been holding. Once inside, she flopped onto the sofa and gave free rein to her warring emotions. Every morning since she had lost Ciarán, she had wanted to find a way to him, but every day had been the same; it was not meant to be. She had finally concluded that only he could travel through time to find her. She had nearly given up hope of going to him until this morning. If another High-lander had found his way here by what seemed like mere chance, it seemed at least possible that someone else might go through the stone chamber as well. She would be that someone.

4

SOMETIME IN WINTER

CIARÁN MACRAE LEANED his head back against the stone wall. He supposed he ought to feel lucky that it was not a dungeon, but he was locked in a castle tower room with no sign of impending release. A chill wind whistled through the gaps in the wrought-iron window frame, coating the walls with a thin layer of frost—the only thing that seemed to thrive in this place. The dark room had been his home for weeks. Porridge and water sustained him, but the memory of love drove him to stay strong just to see her again.

He had been coming home from Mac's world through the stone wall of the chamber when he found himself in the midst of Clan Ross men. When a MacRae landed in their midst, they took it as an attack, and so they seized Ciarán as a prisoner. Luckily they had been spying on the castle and thus had not seen him come through the stone wall behind them. Had they seen such a magical display, they would surely have killed him by now.

Few men knew firsthand about the power of stones. Scattered over Scotland were stone chambers —doorways through time that Ciarán's father and his father before him had spoken of in hushed tones. They had taught Ciarán their ways and about the dangers that one could encounter. Certain chambers had long been destroyed because of the peril that lay beyond. Those that remained were a secret his family had guarded carefully.

Stones. The only stones he saw now were the walls of his room, and they held no magic. He tried to keep track of the days, but what good would it do? Locked in here day after day seemed to render time of little use as a measurement tool. All that mattered was Mac. Would she think of him? Yes, he believed that she would for a time. But they had known one another for mere hours. The memory would fade, and she would one day forget him. How much time might pass until then? That time may already have come.

When had he last seen her? It could have been days ago or a week from now, for when travelers went to the other side, the time could shift. Things were off, sometimes only in small ways, but months could be lost. A man might return a day later to find his own child six months older. The stones were not exact. But he knew he had met her in winter. And when he returned to his realm, snow had dusted the ground. It was on that same day that they had locked him in here.

"Remember me, lassie."

MAC AWOKE with a gasp on a cold Sunday morning. She could still feel Ciarán's kiss on her lips and the touch of his hand on the back of her neck. It was a gentle touch from so rugged a hand. In the time that had passed, her connection to Ciarán had only grown stronger. She could not help but believe that, wherever he was, he was reaching for her. The memory of his face might grow dim, but the rush of pure joy that his presence evoked was too vivid to ever forget. Her memories of him came in flashes—his casual glance, his wry grin, or the glint in his eyes. It was a torment she hoped would not stop, for it made her feel closer to him when she relived those hours in her mind.

How or when love had happened, she could not say precisely. Of course, from the start she had found him wildly attractive. Who wouldn't? The guy was a bundle of muscles and manly assurance, with a kilt to drive home the point. Many men were good-looking, but that was merely a physical aspect that, on its own, was not nearly enough to sway Mac. She had made that mistake only once, and it had taken her longer to recover than she cared to recall. But this man—this Ciarán MacRae—was unlike any man she had known. From then on, she would measure all men against him, and they would fall short, for Ciarán was the one.

The phone rang. Seeing her sister's face on the screen, Mac set the phone down without answering it. She mumbled, "Not now. I'll call you back later." Cam could spoil her good mood after some coffee.

The idea that one perfect mate was fated for each person was a myth—at least, so her sister would tell her. Mac had given up arguing the point years ago. Why try to convince people like her sister of something they've missed when they're happy enough as they are? Before Ciarán, even Mac might have argued that what she felt now was a moment's hormonal reaction. But whatever it was, it was real.

Mac tugged on her jogging suit, looped her hair through a scrunchy, and strode down the road to the chamber for her daily visit.

"It's official. I'm mad. I'm in love with a man who just dropped in from Scotland—eighteenth-century Scotland—and now he has vanished into thin air. Yeah. Nothing crazy about that." Mac rolled her eyes at the sound of her own words. But today she had hope. If yesterday's attacker had come through the stone chamber, then she might be able to go through it, too, and find her way back to Ciarán.

She arrived at the chamber with a fallen tree branch in hand, just in case, and leaned inside. "Hey! Whoever you are, try that again and I'll kick your butt back to your century. So don't mess with me!" When there was no answer or sound, Mac shone her phone's flashlight app inside. Convinced that it was clear, she slipped her phone into her pocket and went to the back of the chamber. As she touched her palm to the stone wall, she felt the loss all over again. "Ciarán," she whispered, "come back." He had been in this spot. Now only stacked stones, rough and cold, stood between them.

He had traveled through time just to see her. He promised that he would return, but he had not told her when.

In the months that followed, Mac wondered if she had succumbed to some sort of hypothermia-induced hallucinations. Had she not met the love of her life? Had she not kissed him? She had relived it all so many times in her mind that she began to wonder whether she had made it all up, or at least part of it. All she knew now, for sure, was that her heart ached from his absence.

5

THE PROMISE

SPRING CAME WITH NO CIARÁN. Not even a wild Highlander came through the stones to threaten her lonely existence. Teaching her kindergarteners was a sort of relief. At least at school she was free from fruitless introspection. Mac busied herself with the routines of work. There was no shortage of ways for a kindergarten teacher to stay occupied. Someone drew her attention each moment. No matter what went on in her personal life, when the first student walked into her room, her mind was fully engaged in instruction, shoe-tying, dispute resolution, safe-keeping, picked scab and nosebleed care, and the myriad of other functions she provided throughout the school day until her small charges were safely aboard their school buses and on their way home.

On the way back inside from escorting her class to the buses, she fell into step beside David.

"Have you ever thought about time travel?" she asked.

He turned and gave a dry look. "You think I'm that much of a nerd?"

"No!" But the look on his face made her grin.

He seemed to take this as an affirmation. "Haven't you got some cardboard bricks and crayons to pick up in your classroom?" He looked ahead and walked on as though she were not there.

"Wait!" Mac caught up to his brisk pace. "David, seriously, what do you know about string theory?"

He stopped in his tracks and looked squarely at her. "String theory?"

She nodded.

"Aren't you pushing your students a bit?"

A broad smile bloomed on her face as she grabbed his arm long enough to give him a proper shove sideways. "It's not for my students."

With a crooked grin, he nodded. "Good. I was beginning to doubt your pedagogical judgment."

A few other teachers were gaining on them and had come within earshot.

"Never mind," Mac said, with a shake of her head.

Minutes later, he popped his head inside her doorway. "String theory?" he said as though twenty minutes had not elapsed since their exchange in the hallway.

Mac stared at him, rethinking her decision to discuss it. He stepped inside and waited for her to respond.

This was crazy, she decided.

David seemed to be in no hurry. He was what some might call a geek, but he was a fit geek because of his cycling hobby. His lean face and pleasant eyes had the look of someone whose thoughts were focused elsewhere. Added to this, his disheveled appearance was topped by dirty-blond hair that landed in straight multidirectional spikes wherever his hand had brushed through it.

"Well?" He stepped closer.

She held his gaze for a very long moment. "Sit down."

He sat on a kindergarten chair across from the kidney-shaped table that served as her desk.

She avoided his gaze. "I was just wondering about time travel. What do you know?"

He peered at her as though she were deranged. Mac shrugged. "Never mind." She then stood and started to leave.

"No, wait."

She shook her head. "It's not important, and I'm sure you've got work to do."

"Not really—other than a small mountain of tests

to grade so I can begin my spring break, but it'll wait."

With dismay, Mac said, "David, I'm sorry. Don't let me keep you."

He tilted his head and squinted. "I'm kidding."

"No, you're not. I've seen your desk."

"Yeah, but that won't change until the last day of school when I get to swipe my arm over my desk and shove what's left on the last day of school into the trash." He grabbed a student-sized chair, folded his lanky frame onto it backward and rested his forearms on the back. "So tell me. What's wrong?"

"I didn't say anything was wrong."

"No, but it is. I know you. Tell me now, or I'll spend my spring break ruminating over the enigma of Mac."

She shook her head. "There's no enigma, just a question."

He gave a nod for her to continue.

"Is it possible?"

"Is what—?"

"Time travel."

"Yes." David paused, concentrating. "But only if you have one of those sports cars. With the doors that lift up." David chuckled.

Mac shut her eyes to hide the eye roll. "Thank you, David. That's all I needed to know." She started to stand.

"In theory, yes, it is possible." He was no longer smiling.

Mac sank back down into her chair.

He leaned forward. "Look, people laugh." He sniffed and made a show of pushing his glasses up his nose. "I've got my image to think of, so I don't talk about stuff like this usually."

Mac looked at him frankly. "Talk to me."

David had the stunned look of someone who had just found his kindred spirit.

Mac pumped him for information without shame. It wasn't as though she hadn't coached him through dozens of dates with various women. Oh, he owed her.

David got up and logged on to Mac's computer. Thirty minutes and a few moans and grunts of interest later, David had shown Mac the prevalent theories, explaining each one with enough detail to make her head spin.

"String theory of course could apply, given the right circumstances. With the right motion and angle, different time periods could coexist. But how would an ordinary person make a journey from one to the other?" He peered at her as though she had the answer.

Mac shook her head and shrugged.

"I don't know either," he continued. "Wormholes make the most sense to me. They're all around us but are too small to see. They could link two different places in two different times."

Mac leaned closer. "So someone could travel from here to a totally different place and time?"

"In theory, but—"

"What if there were wormholes large enough to walk through?" Mac leaned in, gripping the edge of the desk.

David grinned. "What? Just chilling, ready to open like an automatic grocery store door?"

Mac looked away, frowning. "Well, no, not exactly. I just thought there might be places…"

"I doubt it. If there were, people would have done it already, don't you think?"

She nodded. "Yeah, they would have."

David now had the same patient and kind look she had seen him use with his students. "But there aren't. Wormholes are smaller than atoms."

"But they could exist. I mean, it's not entirely impossible." Mac shrugged nonchalantly, which was far from how she was feeling.

"Not impossible—but implausible, yes."

Mac must have looked disappointed because David's attitude shifted. "Look, I'm not saying they exist, because they don't. But if there were human-sized wormholes, there would need to be some sort of energy present, enough to propel someone from one place and time to another. And, of course, they couldn't go any faster than the speed of light."

"Light? Like the sun?"

David's tone became very deliberate, as if he were trying not to sound condescending. "Yeah, the sun emits light."

"And energy? Like solar energy?"

"Yeah, solar energy is a thing." David's brow furrowed. His mouth twitched as though he wanted to smirk, but he kept it in check.

Mac's face lit up. "The sun. It has something to do with the sun."

David's eyes narrowed. "What does?"

Mac pulled herself from her thoughts and looked at him. "Oh. Nothing. Just a book I was reading."

"What book?"

Her eyes darted away as she searched for an answer. "Can't remember."

David's whole demeanor relaxed. "If I'd known you like sci-fi, well, I've got some books you would love."

Before he went on, Mac held up her hand. "No. That's okay. I've got a stack of books at home waiting to be read. I don't need any more, really. But thank you." She shook her head slowly. "So time travel's possible."

"In theory. But no one has tried it—not seriously. Nor will they."

"Why not?"

"Think about it. If you were a brilliant scientist, how crazy would you sound just asking for funding? And then, who would grant it? Time travel research? Game over. Career crash and burn."

"I guess it would sound pretty crazy."

David's smiled faded as he caught something in Mac's expression. "Hey, are you okay?"

She shrugged casually. "Yeah."

David looked toward the door.

"But what if it had already happened?" Mac was serious. "What if someone had done it?"

He met her gaze for a moment and then grinned. "Well, that would be freaking awesome." He laughed. "From the looks of those tests I'm grading, I'm pretty sure my students have time traveled to back before I ever taught them." He stood up. "Well, I'd better get going. Those papers won't grade themselves."

David rose and turned to leave, but Mac barely reacted, still fixed on a thought.

"Well, like I said, I'll be leaving now." With a chuckle, David tapped his fist as though it were a mic. "Is this thing on?"

A smile bloomed on Mac's face. "I'm sorry. I was thinking."

"Yeah, I could tell. I'm intuitive like that. Look, Mac, what's this all about?"

She thought for an instant about telling him, but the next moment she said, "Just curious."

David narrowed his eyes but said nothing.

Mac let out a breath and stood up to follow him to the door. "I'd better let you get back to work."

When he got to the closed door, he turned and extended his hand. "I've had a lovely evening."

Mac laughed and shoved his shoulder as he opened the door and headed back toward his classroom. As she turned back to her desk, her smile faded. What if she could see Ciarán again? Would he still care? Would he even remember her? She thought of her last moments with him—the warmth of his lips and his sure touch as he held her. Could he have forgotten? She had not. Nor would she ever."

6

THE DREAM

Mac's mind raced as she drove along the winding roads leading home. Just before Ciarán had vanished, the sun had shone brilliantly into the cave, but it had glowed from behind him as well. She had thought of it before but dismissed the image as her heart's overreaction to love. The bright light had fit perfectly with the angel choir that should have been there. But as she thought of it now, it made perfect sense. It had been the sun. That was the key to it all, and Ciarán had known it. He had watched the sun rise and had stood in its path when it shone into the chamber.

Her excitement was gone the next instant. If he knew how to do it, then why hadn't he come back to her?

She pulled off to the side of the road and walked to the chamber. The afternoon sun was on the wrong side to shine into the chamber. It must happen only at dawn. She went inside and touched the back wall. *This is crazy. He's not coming back.* She turned and went back to her car. So what if he was from the eighteenth century? Some things never changed. Sure, he found her attractive, but guys were too easily swayed. He was probably sitting right now—or right then—in the eighteenth-century equivalent of a sports bar with some buxom wench on his lap.

"Oh, forget it," she said as she got back into her car and drove down the road. "The main point is, he's gone, and he's not coming back." She pulled into the driveway. *Just suck it up, girl, and drown your sorrows in a pint of frozen fat-filled deliciousness.*

Hours later, an empty cardboard ice cream carton lay on its side, spoon still in it. The TV had gone on to the next film in the lineup, and Mac slept clutching her fluffy pillow and fuzzy blanket.

"MAC, LOVELY MAC. I'M SORRY."

"For what?" she asked with a hint of a smile. Joy shone from her eyes, but sorrow darkened his.

He took her face in his hands. A dim light caught his melancholy expression. "Look around you, my love."

Mac did as he said. They were surrounded by stone walls. It was too large for a stone chamber.

Seeing her confusion, he said, "I'm locked inside here. I cannae come to you, lass."

"But I don't understand. If I got in here to see you, you can come back out with me."

His mouth twitched as though wanting to smile. "Let me look at you, Mac." He reached up, touched her hair gently, and combed his fingers through her hair from the nape of her neck. "Just remember how I love you." He lowered his head, and his lips nearly touched hers. Then, like a vapor, he vanished.

"Wait!" she called into the dark emptiness. "Ciarán!"

STILL ASLEEP, Mac moaned, troubled, but unable to move.

"Mac!" He called to her from so far away.

She tried to cry out, but no sound came. Abruptly, she opened her eyes and sat up. "Ciarán!" She could still feel his presence, as if she might touch him if she reached far enough. "Ciarán, come back to me." But he would not come back. Somehow, he had found his way into her dreams to tell her. He could not come back.

A sliver of light fell on an old book on the shelf:

her mother's collection of Scottish tales. Mac used to curl up with the stories as a girl. Perhaps that was when it began—this love of Scotland and its people. Her favorite was Kenneth MacKenzie, the Brahan Seer. She had often hoped that she, too, might have the second sight he was known for, but the only thing she had ever foreseen was her doom on a college exam. But that had more to do with seeing the inevitable result of procrastination than with seeing the future. She smirked at herself as she picked up the book. Even the Brahan Seer needed help. His second sight came from a stone with a hole in the middle. He would look through the hole and see into the future.

"Right. All I need now is a stone." Mac took in a quick breath as her heart leapt. A stone. A stone with a hole to see into the future. She had always assumed it had been a small, handheld stone, but what if that were more legend than fact? What if the Brahan Seer had not only seen, but also crossed over to the future? What if the legendary stone had actually been a stone chamber like the one Ciarán had passed through? For a brief moment before he was gone, Mac had seen through to the other side as though it were the mouth of another cave. What if the Brahan Seer had done something like that? Could he have been looking through to the other side of a stone chamber?

Mac stood abruptly. Thoughts were flooding her mind. The Brahan Seer's name was MacKenzie, her mother's family name; that was why her mother had named her Mackenzie. What if this had been meant to happen all along? Ciarán could be her soul mate. Mac rolled her eyes. "Whoa, Mac. Talking crazy is one thing, but… soul mate? That's just sappy."

Mac took in a deep breath and then exhaled as she headed for the kitchen. She shook her head. What she needed was some chamomile tea to calm down her wild imagination. There must have been dozens and dozens of people roaming the Highlands with the same name. That did not mean that they all descended from the Brahan Seer. "Drink your tea," she said aloud. "And stop talking to yourself. It's becoming a habit."

For all her years of avoiding commitment, she now felt a tie to a man she had met only once, and she could not deny it. It stretched across time and space. There was something between them—something real. But that was the problem. It all seemed so real. Even her dream had seemed real. What if it had been? What if he had found a way to reach her because he needed her?

"Yeah, sure, that's what happened." She looked up, shaking her head. "But what if?" For a long while, she did not move, focused on thoughts she barely dared to acknowledge. Minutes passed before she surrendered her logic. Love was a force. People sought it, sacrificed for it, and sometimes did terrible things in its name. If the sun had the power to propel people through time, could love's power bond hearts and minds in such a way to connect them through time? The idea cloaked itself over her until she left the kitchen and went to her computer. "I don't care if pretty much everyone I know would think I've lost it. They don't know I'm doing this, and if they don't know, they won't try to stop me."

She emailed David saying she had a family emergency and attached a letter for her principal—just in case she did not make it back before school started again (or at all). She sent another email to Cam telling her she was going on a trip for a while but not to worry. Tears overwhelmed her without warning as she thought about what she was doing. She was going to leave everyone and everything she knew behind to search for a man she had known for one night. Of course, she planned come back, but what if she couldn't? What if she got lost? The stone chamber seemed to lead to one specific place, but how did she know that for sure? What if it sent her to dinosaur times? What if she never found Ciarán?

At that moment, as fear gripped her chest, she heard Ciarán's voice just before they had parted. "Lovely Mac, I will love you, and you will love me." She had believed him then, as she did now. She realized now that, when they had met, he had lived it already. But if that were so, why had he not come back to her since—unless something had happened to him or to his feelings? It was a dark thought that seeped into her mind. But she would not let doubt take root. She could not live life not knowing. He might lie dying or dead or in another's arms, but she would know the truth. She tamped down her fears and thought only of Ciarán's words. They were almost a promise, which she answered in kind. "I will go to you, Ciarán MacRae. I don't know how I will find you, but I will go to you." With that settled, she let out the breath she had been holding. The decision was made. She was going to do it, and the thought gave her peace.

She looked down at herself. She could not exactly wear yoga pants and a cami to eighteenth-century Scotland. She did a quick Internet search to see what women had worn back then. Minutes later, she slid closet hangers aside until she found the only long dress in her closet, a bridesmaid gown. Well, it would have to do. The yoga pants were staying on as part of the ensemble. Men could go commando under their kilts if they liked, but she was going to be warm. She pulled an old hand-knitted sweater from out of a trunk. Her mother had made it for her. It would warm her and, she hoped, not look too out of place. She belted it at the waist and then pulled out a length of wool tartan that her mother had bought while in Scotland on vacation. Her mother had planned to make a duvet cover with it, but then she was gone, and the plaid had remained in Mac's trunk ever since. Mac studied the Internet drawing and did her best to wrap it around her like an airisaid. She then studied herself in the mirror. "The faux silk charmeuse dress looks a bit out of place, but it's better than skinny jeans."

As an afterthought, she grabbed a handmade cloth shoulder bag she had bought at a flea market. She then went to the bathroom, where she filled the bag with a toothbrush and floss, a small tin pillbox (which she loaded with five tablets of antibiotic left over from having strep throat last winter), some aspirin, lip balm, and an emery board. She thought of what else she might need. Some eighteenth-century money would be nice, but she didn't have any lying around, so she'd have to do without. She glanced at the clock. In an hour, it would be dawn. She looked around. She was leaving her home, but she planned to come back. She would have to come back. Her sister would be frantic.

What if her vision of Ciarán in the large stone room had simply been a dream? How could it really have been Ciarán reaching through time to her dreams? Indecision passed as the early morning light caught the gray mist that hung in the air. The world seemed to wait, breathless and enchanted. For what, she did not know. It was the stuff of fairy tales, not real life. Mac shook off her doubts. She might fail, but she would try to reach Ciarán; that was all she could do. Mac faced herself in the mirror. "You can't fail if you don't try." Then she took a deep breath and walked outside.

By the time she reached the stone chamber, sunlight was beginning to burn its way through the fog to the inside of the chamber. Mac went in and stood with her back to the wall, just as Ciarán had stood. Doubt hovered close to the surface. What if she could not find her way to him? But what if she could? If Ciarán had promised to come back, then there must be a way. She clenched her jaw. It was all going to happen. She would make sure it did. That decided, she felt a sudden electric sensation come over her, which she chalked up to fear. It was making her tremble, that was all. She would not give in to it. Again, some sort of current passed through her. Tears moistened her eyes as she stumbled backward, her head swimming. Her balance now lost, she reached for the wall she had been leaning against, but she found herself grasping at air. She was falling when the electrical surge tore through her.

7

TO THE OTHER SIDE

WHEN MAC CAME TO, she was stretched out on the ground, stunned and aching. After a quiet moan, she grumbled the best curse word she could muster. She lay still, afraid that if she moved, something might snap. Ciarán might have warned her about the lightning-like power that would course through her body as she crossed into the past. She had somehow formed the impression that it would be like stepping on and off an escalator. Right.

There she lay on the ground, not quite ready to move, and she opened her eyes. Light shone into the cave. A stab of panic shot through her as she looked around for wild Scotsmen on the attack, but she was alone. Still trembling from the force of the power that had gone through her minutes before, she took care getting up. Once upright, she determined that

nothing seemed damaged. She took in a deep breath
and was struck by the scent of early spring grasses
mixed with damp stones and earth. Outside, a single
bird sang out, unanswered. When she reached the
mouth of the cave, Mac could see a castle in the
distance. She recognized it more because of its setting
than because she'd actually seen it before. Eilean
Donan Castle. The sight took her breath. Her mother,
proud MacKenzie that she was, had shown her
pictures in books and told family stories passed down
through the generations. Mac now wished she had
paid better attention.

It was either early morning or late afternoon, for
the sun was quite low in the sky. Mac crept out of the
cave. She would head for the castle, where she hoped
to find Ciarán. She had nothing to go on but logic. If
Ciarán had traveled through the stones here, there
was a good chance that he would be nearby. He was a
MacRae. He had told her that much. Although the
MacKenzies owned the castle, their close allies, the
MacRaes, lived there as constables. Even if Ciarán
was not there, someone would know where he was.
They might not trust her enough to tell her, but it was
her best option.

So Mac set out for the castle. She cursed as she
dragged her skirt through some sort of dropping—
horse or cow, from the size of it. Wiping what she
could on the grass, she muttered, "It's summer camp

all over again. I sucked at nature back then, and I suck at it now. If only I'd signed up for *Mountain Miss Adventures* instead of *Jazz Hands on Deck*."

The distance was farther to walk than it had looked from the cave. She could jog it, if only it were a flat surface, but the terrain was rough and uneven, with spongy patches that threatened to throw her off-balance. The last thing she needed was a twisted ankle. She missed her trail runners—not that she ever ran trails in them, but they had been great on her summer vacation for walking down Edinburgh's cobbled streets. It was too bad they would have looked out of place here. Despite her best efforts, she was sure she already looked strange enough.

When she reached the shore of the loch, she knelt down to drink water from cupped hands. After she finished, she looked across the water to the castle. Whichever MacRae had rebuilt the castle in the early 1900s had been a genius to build a bridge. Now, in the eighteenth century, there was no way to get there but over the water. She would have to swim to the island, which wouldn't have been so bad in a swimsuit, but in the bulky clothing she had on, it might be a challenge. She bent down and pulled the back of her skirt hem between her legs to the front and tucked it over her belt. With one last look at the castle, she stepped into the water.

And back out she came, kicking as strong arms

pulled her by the waist. She was plopped onto dry land, but one arm remained hooked around her chest from behind and the other around her hips, making movement nearly impossible. A deep, gravelly voice near her ear said, "What d'ye think you're doing?"

"Swimming," Mac said, trying to mask her fear with her best display of anger.

Her captor chuckled. "Well, you're not in the water, so you might as well stop that kicking."

She did not. In fact, despite the man's tight grip, Mac managed to work her hand over to just the right place to grasp hold of his bollocks and twist.

With a guttural cry, he released her with a shove that sent her to the ground on all fours. "The wee devil!"

While the one man gripped his groin, another one let out a hearty laugh.

Mac scrambled to her feet, but a hand grasped her upper arm and held on like a vise before she could run. "She's quite bonnie for a devil."

"You may have her," said the first. "As you've no bollocks to lose."

"'Tis not what your wife says."

Mac rolled her eyes. "Really?"

"Pay my friend Fergus no heed," the second man spoke softly into her ear.

Mac thrashed about in his grip.

"Calm yourself, girl."

She jerked her shoulders angrily. "Calm myself— when you're holding me captive? And don't call me 'girl.'" Mac tried to sound strong, but she quavered inside.

Now somewhat recovered, Fergus said, "Hold her hands, Hamish." Fergus then wrapped a length of rope around Mac's wrists and, with a final yank, tightened and tied them together behind her back.

Hamish loosened his grip enough for Mac to jerk her arm free of his grasp and take off in a run. Hamish and Fergus exchanged weary looks, and then Hamish set out after Mac. His long limbs made chasing her easy enough, but the job was made even easier when the uneven ground caught her foot, causing her to fall face first. Boggy ground cushioned her fall, leaving only her spirit wounded and her face slathered in mud.

Mac sat up and was working her way to her feet when Hamish slipped his arms under hers and lifted her in one swift motion. She considered her options. Running had not worked out well. Even if she managed to free herself again, there was no place to hide. She decided to save her strength for a better opportunity.

Hamish smeared the worst of the mud from her face. "Are you hurt?" A warm look with a tinge of amusement shone in his eyes.

Mac found this reassuring—if not to the point of

complete trust, then at least to a point at which she did not fear for her life—at least not for the moment.

Hamish said, "You'd best tell us your name and your business here, lass, for I'm losing my patience."

Thoughts raced through her mind as she tried to decide how to answer. Clan tartans would not come into use for a hundred more years, so she could not tell by their plaid who they were. With the castle so close, the odds were better that these men were MacKenzies or MacRaes, which would make them Ciarán's clansmen. On the other hand, they could be spies, in which case she did not need to volunteer that she was a MacKenzie. "I am…"

As Fergus joined them, leading two horses by the reins, Mac feigned distraction in an effort to stall giving the inevitable answer. But the two men exchanged a look that Mac read to mean that her time was just about up. However, she could not get past the fact that her given name would not pass as such in these times, assuming these times were anytime before the twentieth century (which, judging from their plaids, horses, and apparent lack of deodorant, she felt safe in assuming).

Fergus drew close and peered into her eyes. "She's either forgotten her name, or she's a Ross."

Mac heaved a sigh. "Oh, all right. It's Mackenzie."

"MacKenzie?" said Fergus.

"Yes."

"And your forename?" asked Hamish.

"Mac. People just call me Mac."

"'Tis not a proper name for a woman."

With a helpless shrug, Mac said, "So I've been told."

"And your purpose?"

Mac's emotions welled up inside. She was in a strange place. Two brawny Scotsmen held her at their mercy, and her feelings for Ciarán seemed so far removed from her time or his that she wondered if she had made a mistake. He had kissed her. So what? A kiss wasn't exactly a lasting commitment. Would he even remember or care for her now? "I'm not sure anymore." As she said it, tears moistened her eyes.

She was too busy loathing herself for her show of emotion to see the two men exchange looks. Her nose was beginning to run.

Hamish asked, "If I let go of you, will you run?"

"Yes."

He chuckled. "Well, then, I'll have to hold onto you, won't I?" He turned to Fergus. "I suppose we should take her to the castle."

Mac's ears perked at the mention of the castle.

With a shake of his head, Fergus said, "We've already wasted enough time on this girl. I say we tie her and leave her here for someone to find later."

Fergus meant it. Mac had no doubt of that, but

she caught Hamish's look of disapproval, which gave her hope. She might have been making a fatal mistake, but the thought of being left tied up on the moor frightened her more than being in the custody of these two. Something about Hamish made her want to trust him. He was younger and seemed far less cynical than his companion. Even Fergus, as weathered and harsh as he was, did not seem a cruel man, so Mac took a chance and blurted out, "I came to find Ciarán MacRae."

Hamish's grip tightened at the sound of the name. "Ciarán?"

Fergus's eyes glimmered sharply against his leather skin.

Mac tried to glance over her shoulder, but she could not get a good look at Hamish. Unable to read their reactions, Mac had little choice but to forge on and ask, "Do you know him?"

"The question is," said Fergus, "how do you know him?"

"I met him one night in a storm."

"Met him? When?"

"I couldn't tell you exactly. I knew him for only a day."

Hamish peered at her thoughtfully. "After knowing him for one day, you appear in our midst. From the looks of you, I'd wager you arenae from here. And you sound very strange."

"Strange, indeed," chimed in Fergus.

Mac could not help the look of annoyance she threw Fergus's way.

Hamish drew her attention back. "Why would you come all the way here looking for Ciarán?" With a sideways glance at Fergus, Hamish moved closer to Mac. Now inches away, he said softly, "You love him."

"No!" Mac protested. "How could I? I barely know him."

Fergus narrowed his gaze. "You're with child."

Mac shot him another look of annoyance. "Not that it's any business of yours, but no—and thanks for making me feel like a cow."

"Och, but you're a bonnie cow. Is she not, Fergus?" Hamish whisked a lingering trace of dried mud from Mac's face. "Easy, lass. Ciarán is being held for ransom at Balnagown Castle, and he is my brother."

Mac's head was reeling. "You're his brother. He's locked up in a castle? What happened? Why aren't you getting him out?"

"We were going to do just that when we came upon you."

"Well, let's go! Tell me more on the way." She turned around. "Please untie me. This is just wasting time."

Fergus mounted his horse. "No, lass. You're staying here. Hamish, just leave her."

Mac gave Hamish a pleading look. "No. Please. I've got to see him."

Fergus said, "There's no time to take her back to the castle."

"But we could send her back whence she came." Hamish's knowing expression made Mac suspect that he knew all about the stone chamber and perhaps about her. He quietly said, "Go home, lass. 'Tis not safe for you here. I'll tell Ciarán I saw you. He can come to you if we're able to free him."

"If? I have waited for months. There's no 'if' about it."

"I'm sorry."

"Hamish," said Fergus, with a growl of impatience.

"Home is the best place for you, lassie." With that, Hamish bade Mac good-bye and turned away. After mounting his horse, he and Fergus rode off, leaving Mac standing alone.

8

THE CROSSROADS

As HAMISH and Fergus disappeared over the horizon, Mac wondered whether she should follow their trail or simply go home. "As if I even know how to follow a trail." She let out a deep sigh. She was losing this round of "Girl versus Highlands." What next? She could press on, but for what? For a guy who had kissed her and told her he would love her? She could find that at any singles bar in the New York metro area. Mac looked back toward the chamber with a sigh. It was too late to do anything now. If her theory was right, the stone chamber would take her back home in the morning, assuming the dawn sunlight shone into both sides of the chamber, past and present. So all she had to do was to spend the night here and go home in the morning. It was, by far, the most sensible choice.

Or she could walk. She could follow their trail until it ended at Balnagown Castle or until she lost them completely. What then? It was not as if she could check her GPS or pull over to a service station and ask for directions. A person might go for miles without seeing someone else. Mac knew herself well. She was smart; she worked hard; she was good with small children; and she sucked at navigating. There was a good chance she'd get lost on the way, and then where would she be? Well, that was the point; she wouldn't know.

The far safer plan was to wait here until the men came back with Ciarán—if they came back with Ciarán. And yet that was the plan she could not execute. Waiting here would be torment, as would be going home without knowing Ciarán's fate. If the roles were reversed, he would try to help her—even if he had to ride on horseback down I-684 at rush hour to find her. Mac could do no less than Ciarán would do.

And so she decided to go after Ciarán alone, if only to see him one last time. But one last time before what? A chill shot through her. She would not think like that. All her effort would go toward finding Ciarán. The rest would wait until then. Mac stood up, brushed herself off, and set out toward the direction the men had gone.

It had recently rained, so their trail would be easy

to follow. Her modern length of tartan was a much finer weave than the cloth from this time and not nearly as warm as Ciarán's plaid had felt during their one night together. She sighed as she thought of how warm she had felt in his arms.

A horseman appeared up ahead. Adrenaline shot through Mac's chest as she thought about what to do next. As she hiked up her skirt and started to run for a tree to try to hide, a deep voice called out, "Mac!"

It was Hamish. He had come back for her. Mac walked toward him, full of hope that she could not suppress. After bringing his horse to a halt beside her, Hamish reached down. "Come, lass."

Until now, she had not seen the resemblance. But in this kind gesture, she saw traces of Ciarán. Hamish had a stockier build and red hair that was wild about his face, but his eyes, at that moment, were Ciarán's. Warm and reassuring, he made her feel safe and a little bit homesick. She swallowed her emotions and grasped Hamish's hand as he pulled her up behind him.

"Hang on, and I'll take you to Ciarán."

THEY CAUGHT up to Fergus and rode in silence all morning until they arrived at a stream, where they stopped to rest and water the horses. While Fergus went off to relieve himself, Hamish started a fire. "So you love him, then?"

Mac flinched as he broke the silence but quickly recovered. "Love him? I barely know him." She met Hamish's questioning look with a mischievous twinkle in her eyes. "I thought you meant Fergus."

After surprise crossed over his face, Hamish let out a laugh.

Mac let the spark in her eyes spread to a full grin.

When his laughter subsided, Hamish said, "And what of Ciarán?"

Mac blinked. "You're his brother. You know more about him than I do."

With a quick look of appraisal, Hamish said, "You love him."

Her evasive tactic having failed, Mac worked to refute it. "We just spent the one night together."

Hamish lifted an eyebrow.

"Not like you're thinking," Mac went on. "No, we were forced to seek shelter together."

With a roguish look, Hamish nodded. "Shelter."

"Yes, shelter. It was a snowstorm—a bad one."

He nodded deliberately. "Oh, aye."

"Aye—yes," she insisted. "All there was between us was a kiss." Her mouth turned up in an unexpected smile as she recalled it. Her eyes flitted up to find Hamish grinning, and they flitted back down to avoid him. "It was a good-bye kiss."

"Oh, I think he would have told me about that."

Mac bristled. "Are you saying I'm lying?"

"No, lass. Calm yourself. I only mean that they must have caught him before he had a chance to come home."

"Oh. Sorry."

He gave her an admiring look. "For I'm certain he would have told me about meeting someone like you."

"Would he?" Mac hated to let down her guard to reveal her true feelings, but she could not help but wonder. "I would think someone like Ciarán would have his pick of young ladies." Mac inwardly groaned. When had she become that woman?

A sly spark lit Hamish's eyes. "Aye, he does."

As if coyly fishing for information had not been enough, now she had to hide her disappointment with the results. Of course he had women around him. He was strong and attractive—if attractive meant heart-hammeringly hot—and he was kind. Who would ever want that? Mac's eyes closed as she exhaled. This was a fool's errand. She looked up to find Hamish studying her with merciful eyes.

"Dinnae *fash yersel*, lass. He'll have none of them."

And he may not want me. It was all she could do not to voice it. Even so, Hamish seemed to understand.

"I dinnae ken Ciarán's mind, but I will tell you this: We'll make certain you have a chance to find out."

"How, by abandoning me in the middle of nowhere?"

Hamish waved dismissively. "*Och*, one of the men would have found you and taken you into the castle. This is part of their regular patrol."

"Thanks for letting me know." Mac looked away to spare him the full force of her glare. "So what changed your mind?"

He leaned closer and lowered his voice. "Love. But dinnae tell Fergus. He'll think I've gone soft." A corner of his mouth twitched in a way she had seen Ciarán's do.

"Love?"

"Aye. I could see that you love him, and I couldnae see how he couldnae love you."

Mac felt herself blush. "Why, Hamish, I think you have gone soft."

He got up abruptly and said gruffly, "Dinnae grow used to it, lass."

Mac suppressed the broad smile that sought to be free. "I wouldn't think of it, Hamish."

"And dinnae worry Fergus with talk of such things."

"Such things?"

Hamish cleared his throat. "He didnae want a lass trailing along."

"Trailing?"

Hamish shrugged. "He thought you might slow us down."

Mac bristled. "Oh, great. So Fergus hates me."

"Not at all. He just doesn't want a girl to look after."

"What—does he think I'll slow you down by stopping to fix my mascara?"

"Mascara?"

"Eye makeup."

Hamish frowned in confusion.

Mac smirked. "Never mind. I'll be fine."

Hamish did not dismiss it so easily. "Lass, you must promise to do as I say. We're riding into danger, and our ways are strange to you yet. Stay close and mind me."

Although Fergus kept his footfalls silent, his figure was still visible as he came back from the other side of the hill. In a low voice, Hamish said, "Dinnae speak of the stone chambers."

Mac's jaw fell slack.

Hamish looked gravely into her eyes. "I ken how you got here. 'Tis a family secret, and it must remain so."

"But—"

He glanced toward Fergus, who was quickly approaching. "*Whisht!* We'll not talk of it now."

Fergus joined them with three salmon, scaled and gutted, hanging from a horsehair line. He stuck them each on a wet stick and handed one each to Hamish and Mac to hold over the fire.

Hamish spoke to Mac as if continuing from where he'd left off. "Before we found you, a messenger came from Clan Ross to tell us they'd captured Ciarán. It seems they came onto our lands and lay in wait until they could find one of us to ransom."

"One of us?"

"I'm the Constable of Eilean Donan, and Ciarán would take over in my absence. I'm sure Clan Ross would rather have me, but they found Ciarán first, and they knew I would pay for his freedom."

"Except that you didn't," said Mac.

The corner of Hamish's mouth twitched. "We don't want to appear too eager lest they ask for more ransom."

Mac nodded. "And Ciarán's safety and comfort mean nothing?"

Hamish shrugged indifferently. "*Och!* Comfort."

"Yes, comfort. You can't just leave him there for weeks on end."

Hamish studied Mac. "Men must have grown very soft in your time."

Mac's jaw dropped. She had no retort. Compared to the men of this time, one could make a good case that by eighteenth-century Highland standards, twenty-first-century men were soft, in the sense that they enjoyed central heat and air and the occasional overpriced coffee. She was in Hamish's time now, so she abandoned the point with a sigh. "Never mind."

Turning her thoughts back to Ciarán, she pieced together what must have happened. The men from Clan Ross had caught him as he had returned from seeing her. If his journey through the stone chamber had been anything like hers, they might have found him passed out on the ground, helpless to defend himself until it was too late.

"What will they do to him?" Mac asked, afraid for the answer.

"*Och*, they'll lock him away and wait for us to come. By the time we arrive, they'll have tired of playing this game and will accept what we offer for ransom."

"And if they don't?"

"We'll do something else."

Mac gave up trying to look patient. "Something else. This ought to be good."

Hamish smiled at her for a little too long. He swept his fingers through his long strands of hair.

Before Hamish could speak, Fergus said, "Help him escape. You could do it."

Mac drew back in surprise. "Me?"

Fergus had addressed her directly. It must have pained him to do so. Mac was unsure of how to react, but her curiosity led the way. "So you want me to rescue him"—as she said it, she realized Hamish's reason and nodded—"to avoid paying the ransom." She glared for a moment then looked away and said softly, "Cheap bastard."

Hamish shrugged. "We've got better use for the money."

"Better use than freeing your brother?"

"Aye."

"I don't know what's worse, your tight fist or your arrogance."

"Oh, my fist, by far."

Mac lifted her chin. "Are you threatening me?"

"Why would I bother?"

This annoyed Mac even more.

Seeing her frustration, Hamish said, "Lass. Dinnae *fash*. I'll not harm you, nor will anyone else."

"And what about Ciarán? Can you promise that no one will harm him—if they haven't already?"

Hamish looked at Mac as though she were the one with the problem. "Calm yourself, woman. Ciarán's a strong lad. He'll take care of himself. We're on our way to him, are we not?"

"Yes, and I finally see why you came back for me." Mac rolled her eyes and looked away.

Hamish ignored her as he pulled his salmon from the fire and started to eat.

Fergus muttered to Hamish, "She's a wee bit high-strung, that one."

"I heard that," said Mac. "Look, Fergus, you can stop trying to convince me that you hate me. I get it."

Fergus gave Hamish a questioning look and then turned his attention to the fish. He rotated it and then pulled it from the fire and offered it, skewer and all, to Mac.

She eyed him suspiciously. "Thank you."

When he went on and ate with no more than a glance, Mac decided to do the same. Unsure of how to eat it, she reasoned that it would not do to eat it like a corn dog, so she gently slid the meat off in bite-sized pieces with her fingertips. After a minute of unnatural silence, Mac looked up to find the men watching her with looks of suppressed amusement before returning to their food, which they bit off in large chunks from the sticks.

She looked away and murmured to herself, "What's that, Fergus, a smile? That must have hurt."

After they had all finished eating in silence, Mac looked around, searching for anything that might serve as a napkin. She soon gave up and wiped her hands on her skirt. When she was done, she turned to the men. "So, gentlemen." She was not going to let them get the better of her. If she could manage obstinate five-year-olds, she could manage a crusty old Scot and his constable. "You must have a plan. What is it?"

9

TO BALNAGOWN CASTLE

BALNAGOWN CASTLE LOOKED wondrous and grand until Mac remind herself that the man whom she thought she might love was a prisoner there. Having been warned that Clan Ross would be watching, she proceeded on foot all alone. When a guard stopped her at the gatehouse, she told him she was looking for work.

"What sort of work?"

Judging from the look in his eyes, he seemed to have something in mind, but Mac did her best to ignore it. She had another sort of work in mind, for Hamish had told her that one of the kitchen maids had recently come down with a stomach ailment after spending some time in the tavern with him.

Mac said, "I've been a dairymaid and a cook's

helper." She paused and watched his eyes travel the length and the breadth of her slowly.

"Go inquire over there at the kitchen." He tilted his head to indicate where. "I'll come along later to see how you fare." His lips spread into a smile.

Mac lowered her eyes as she curtsied and moved on. The guard turned and watched her walk away for a moment before he was torn away to resume his duties.

Mac arrived at the kitchen to find it aflutter. She stopped at the doorway and tried to get someone's attention. Having no success, she took a step inside. The cook saw her and said, "Not now. Can't you see that we're busy?"

"I was told you needed help."

The cook sized her up in seconds and thrust a large basket at her. "Take this out to the garden and fetch some turnips and kale."

Mac nodded, concealing her stunned reaction, and took the basket. It was the shortest job interview she had ever had. A few inquiries got her out to the vegetable garden. "Excuse me, sir," she asked a man she assumed was the gardener. "Which row is the kale?"

He rolled his eyes and then nodded toward a row of curly green leaves and went on with his work. After filling her basket, Mac went back to the kitchen.

As the evening wore on, she wore out. It was

grueling work, and as fit as she once thought she was, she was no match for eighteenth-century kitchen labor. When she was at last permitted to rest, she was given a plate of food to eat outside in the twilight. She had eaten but half when the cook came to the doorway. "Take this to the room at the top of the tower."

One of the kitchen maids took in a sharp breath and then crossed herself. Seeing this, Mac asked, "What is it?"

The maid's eyes darted toward the cook but then returned to her work, taking great pains to avoid Mac's gaze again.

Before she could inquire further, the cook thrust a tray at Mac, saying, "Dinnae be all day about it."

"Aye, mistress."

At the top of the stairway, Mac paused. There was no one around. She did not need to ask where to deliver the food, for there was only one door. It was locked. "Hello?" she called.

Someone stirred from the other side of the door. "Aye." The voice was deep but ragged.

"I've your dinner here for you." She had been told to slide the tray under the door. There was a space of just a few inches between the door and stone floor. Mac set down the tray and did as she had been told.

The cloth cover slid off to reveal a thick slice of bread and a shallow bowl of water, there being no room for a cup to pass under the door. A hand shot through the gap and clutched hers, and she gasped. The grip tightened.

"Please, sir. I was told to be quick."

"You've a strange sort of speech. From whence come you?"

Mac tried to wriggle free, but he was too strong.

"I said, where are you from?"

Mac turned her ear toward the sound of his voice, but she could not be sure. "Far away, sir." Loud footsteps sounded from the stairway. Mac looked but saw no one.

"Mac?" said the voice from the other side of the door.

"Ciarán!"

He loosened his grip on her hand. Then he put his other hand over hers and tenderly stroked the inside of her palm and wrist.

She smiled, thrilled by the touch of his hand stroking hers.

"What are you doing here, lass? How on earth did you find me?"

"We've come to bring you home."

"We?"

In a futile effort to draw nearer, Mac reached her other hand under the door, desperate to touch him as much as she could while they hurried to whisper all that was on their minds and their hearts. "Hamish and Fergus are with me."

"God's teeth, lass, how did you come upon them?"

"Remind me to tell you that later. Right now, I need to know who has the key to this door."

"I dinnae ken, lass."

"Okay. I'll try to find out." She pressed her cheek to the door as though it might bring her closer to him.

Ciarán's voice caught in his throat. "It isnae safe for you here in the castle. Hamish shouldnae have allowed it."

"I insisted."

"And he let you. I'll have words with him when I see him again."

"Don't blame him, Ciarán. I had to."

"*Och*, Mac."

"It's your fault. If you weren't such a good kisser, I might not have."

He tried to laugh, which was what she wanted him to do, but their feelings were too deeply rooted. His grip tightened around her hand.

Mac squeezed his hand in response. Hasty footsteps drew near. Mac looked but still saw no one. "I work in the kitchen, so I'm not far away. I'll come back as soon as I can."

She screamed as a hand gripped her rump and then pulled at her hips. Her hands were pulled from Ciarán's grasp, but she gripped the bottom of the door with her fingertips. Ready to kick and fight off her attacker, she turned. But no one was there.

Ciarán's voice was frantic as he reached under the door. "Mac!"

"I'm okay." Her voice was breathless. She stood and searched the hall, pulling aside tapestries to make sure they were alone. But her fearful panting betrayed her. "Someone touched me, but no one is here." She reached under the door for his hand. "I've got to go, but I'll be back soon. I promise."

He gave her hand a squeeze. "Be careful, lass."

"I promise I will." She squeezed his hand in return and then hurried back down the stairs, her heart still pounding.

All eyes were on her as she came into the kitchen. It made her uneasy.

The cook asked, "Are you all right?"

"Yes," she lied. "Why wouldn't I be?"

"No reason."

With that, everyone returned to their duties.

Mac started helping one of the girls make some oatcakes. "What is it? Tell me."

"I dinnae ken what you mean," said the girl. She could not have been more than thirteen or fourteen, and she blushed far too easily.

"You've seen him, haven't you?"

The girl's eyes opened wider. "Seen who? I dinnae ken what you mean."

"Yes, you do. Tell me." Mac looked her straight in

the eye until she glanced around to make sure no one was looking. Finally she gave a weak nod.

"Who's up there?" asked Mac.

"*Och*, no! Did he do something to you?"

Mac gave a slight nod. "He touched me. Who is he?"

"Did you see him?"

"No, I just felt him—or rather, he felt me."

Now overwhelmed by sympathy, the girl leaned closer and said in hushed tones, "Black Andrew."

"Black Andrew? But how could he have climbed up that narrow stairway and then just disappeared?"

The maid whispered, "Because he isnae a man; he's a ghost."

A week ago, Mac would have laughed, but too much had happened since then that no one would believe. Ghost or not, she had felt creepy hands groping her bottom. With a shudder, she had to admit to herself that she believed in Black Andrew. But she believed in Ciarán more, so she would do what she must to save him—even if she had to go through Black Andrew to do it.

When darkness fell and her work was done, Mac went to find Hamish and Fergus behind the stables, where they had agreed to meet. They had secured lodgings outside the castle, in a small byre with hay for a mattress. They produced an extra plaid for Mac to use as a blanket since the length of tartan she had brought with her was too fine to provide her the warmth she would need on a chilly summer night in the Highlands.

After talking through what information and supplies they would need to free Ciarán, they settled into their sleeping arrangements. As they had been all along, the two men were perfect, if awkward, gentlemen. At this point, Mac was simply too tired to care where she slept. Drained by her first day of work as a kitchen maid, Mac made her bed with her two pieces of plaid and settled down for a welcome night's sleep.

As she lay there, a thought worried her. "How will I know it is time to get up?"

Fergus mumbled, "I'll wake you, lass."

"But how will you know?" It seemed a fair question to Mac.

"*Och*, he'll know," Hamish said. "Go to sleep."

"Okay." She lay still, unable to sleep, and breathed in the close air of the byre. It smelled just as a byre should. Mac accepted this without complaint, but doing so did not make breathing any easier. To distract herself, she turned her thoughts to the next day. "Guys—uh, lads?"

"Aye?" Hamish grumbled.

"The castle is haunted."

"Aye?" Fergus said, with a yawn.

"He touched me."

"Black Andrew?" asked Hamish.

"Wait. You knew about Black Andrew, but you sent me in anyway?"

Ignoring her question, Hamish asked, "How did he touch you?"

"With a lot of enthusiasm."

"That's not what I meant."

"I know what you meant."

Mac could hear the smile in Hamish's voice as he said, "So he's friendly, then?"

"Not exactly."

"Are you sure it was a ghost? Maybe one of the guards—"

"I think I would know if a guard snuck up behind me." Her biting tone silenced both men. "And if he were a man, I'd have felt something when I kicked him in the crotch, but I didn't, because no one was there."

Hamish spoke slowly, with reluctance. "So the stories are true."

"Yeah, next time maybe you could share them with me."

"I didnae think they were real."

Mac's glare was lost in the darkness. "What stories? You owe me that much."

Fergus chimed in. "Oh, there once was a laird who forced himself on the women until one day the people attacked him and hanged him outside the room at the top of the tower."

"You mean the room where Ciarán is." Mac exhaled. "Thanks. Good to know."

Fergus's breathing grew measured and loud. After long moments of quiet, Mac thought Hamish had fallen asleep as well, but he said, "Are you going to be all right? 'Tis not too late to change your mind."

"No, I came here to help you free Ciarán, and that's what I'll do."

"There's a good lass. Now get some sleep."

10

A SIMPLE PLAN

In the morning, Mac arrived at the castle with the sole objective of finding the key to Ciarán's room. Once she did, Hamish and Fergus would find fresh clothing and a razor for Mac to slip under the door to Ciarán. His full, untrimmed growth of beard would make him easy to spot if Clan Ross discovered him missing, so he would trim his beard to blend in with the visiting merchants on market day, when he would make his escape. The plan was a simple one. Mac would unlock the door and lead Ciarán out of the castle to meet with Hamish and Fergus. From there, Mac and Hamish would create a diversion so Fergus and Ciarán could slip past the guards at the gate. As long as Ciarán's escape went undiscovered, the guards would be more concerned about who came into the castle than who came out. But all of it hinged upon finding the key to get Ciarán out of the locked room.

At work in the kitchen, Mac was instructed to help Ailis, another kitchen maid, prepare a breakfast tray. Mac set down some fresh milk she had just brought in from the byre. "For a prisoner, he's fed very well."

With barely a glance, Ailis said, "Aye, well, he's highborn, so I suppose they're only keeping him until they can get a ransom. 'Tis not like he's a common thief, is it?"

"For ransom? So if someone from his clan paid his ransom, they would simply set him free?"

"Oh, aye." Ailis smiled as though anyone should have known this.

Mac was troubled. If all Hamish had to do was pay a ransom to set Ciarán free, then he either did not have the money or did not wish to part with the money for the sake of his brother. She forced herself to set aside thoughts of Hamish. There was nothing she could do about that now. Ciarán needed her now, so she would focus on how she could best help Ciarán, which was to find that key. With the tray now nearly ready, she said, "What does he look like? Has anyone seen him?"

Ailis lifted her eyes to meet Mac's, and a smile bloomed on her face. She leaned closer. "*Och*, he's a braw lad."

"So you saw him?"

"Aye."

"Did you go to his room all by yourself?" Mac asked, returning a conspiratorial smile. The razor for him to shave was definitely essential to the plan now. At least Ailis had seen him, and no doubt there were others.

"*Och*, no. A guard came with me."

"If he's as braw as you say, I'd like to see him. Perhaps I could go next time."

Ailis's brow wrinkled. "Oh, I dinnae ken about that. Besides, they only unlock the door every sennight to empty his chamber pot."

Mac thought of a chamber pot being left in the room for a week, and her nose wrinkled reflexively. Ailis laughed.

Mac's eyes brightened. "I could come with you!"

"Oh, I dinnae think you could do that."

"It's your fault, Ailis. After hearing you describe him, who could blame me for wanting to see him?"

Ailis grinned. "No one who's seen him would blame you."

"What if," Mac said slowly, as though forming the thought for the first time, "you took me along as part of my training?"

"Your what?"

"To teach me how to do it, just in case you're needed elsewhere—for something more important— or if you were ill."

"Well, Cook promised me she would let me help out cooking. I dinnae want to be fetching milk and delivering trays for the rest of my life. I want to better myself."

Mac nodded. "So do I. So you understand."

"Aye, but it's not me you'll have to convince."

Four days and a good deal of convincing, later, Mac was thanking her college psychology instructor and five years of managing classroom behavior for giving her the skills to convince the cook that she needed more help. That, alone, was not hard to accomplish. But Mac sang Ailis's praises so well that the cook soon saw Ailis as the ideal assistant. Of course, someone would need to be trained to attend to the prisoner's room when Ailis was busy with more important duties in the kitchen.

By the time they made their next trip up the stairs, the cook thought it had all been her idea. Carrying a tray of food once more, Mac followed Ailis and one of the guards to the room at the top of the tower. While they waited for the guard to find the right key, Ailis rattled off chores they would do once inside. Bedding would be shaken out the window and the bed remade. The chamber pot would be carried to the garderobe to be emptied and returned to the room. Mac did her best to look attentive even as her mind raced through what was to come. Once inside, the guard left them to their work while he waited outside the door.

"Oh! I've forgotten the milk!" Mac said, looking at Ailis with pleading eyes. "Would you mind? My back has been hurting terribly today. I must have hurt it carrying that last cask of ale." That was not altogether a lie.

Ailis did not look pleased, but, as she opened her mouth to protest, she glanced at Ciarán and suppressed her true reaction. "Oh, I suppose I could get it." When she got to the doorway where Ciarán could not see her, she scowled at Mac.

Mac smiled sweetly as she pulled the door closed —well, almost closed. She exchanged looks with Ciarán and proceeded to fluff up the straw-filled mattress. In a stage voice, she said, "I'll just be a moment, and then you can sit down."

By the time she had finished her sentence, Ciarán had yanked open the door, pulled the guard into the room by the neck, and landed a blow that knocked the flailing man out cold. Ciarán then traded clothes with him, and they left the guard locked in the room.

Ciarán flashed a winning grin and made a grand bow, and then he gestured toward the stairwell. "Shall we?"

Mac smiled and turned toward the stairs, but Ciarán swept her into his arms and kissed her. He released her with a guttural sound of frustration. "Off with you now, before I do something we'll both regret —but enjoy."

Mac tried to ignore the thrill that went through her as she grinned and heaved a huge sigh. "Very well, sir."

"You sound a bit Scottish."

Mac smiled proudly. "I've been working on it. People still look at me strangely, but I'm making an effort."

Mac rounded the last curve in the stairs and nearly bumped into Ailis. "Oh, Ailis! I saw him again!"

"Who?"

Ailis shifted her weight to the side of the narrow spiral staircase, but Mac did not move. Ailis could not proceed.

Mac opened her eyes wide and gasped. "The ghost! Black Andrew! He assaulted me!"

"No!" Ailis took no convincing. She thrust the milk into Mac's hands. "Here. Take it up to him later. I've work in the kitchen!" She turned and could not scurry down the stairs fast enough.

Mac led the way down and waited until everyone was distracted enough to lead Ciarán to the outside door, ditching the milk along the way. Ciarán squinted in the bright sunlight, but Mac hooked her arm into his and led him away, leaving behind the rest of the castle in a flurry of midmorning activity.

When they passed a large tree, Mac paused and leaned against it, trying to steady her trembling hands.

His eyes now accustomed to the light, Ciarán gave Mac's arm a light squeeze. "Steady, lass." He clasped her hand, kissed her forehead, and led her through the bailey. It was market day, and the bailey was filled with pushcarts, merchants, and folk ready to haggle and shop. Few would recognize Ciarán because he had been locked away since his arrival. Even so, Mac was nervous. She led him to the outskirts of the market, where Hamish was waiting with a horse and a cart.

As the brothers embraced, Mac asked, "What's this?"

"Ciarán would do better to hide in the cart as we pass through the gate."

"But our plan—"

"Will proceed. All that's new is the cart."

"Your carriage, my lord." Hamish gestured for Ciarán to get in. Ciarán didn't comply right away but instead curled his body around Mac's while Hamish filled the cart with empty baskets and covered it all with an oilcloth. Once that was done, he got in and hid himself among the baskets.

Mac walked ahead of the cart and approached the guard with an engaging smile.

"'Tis a fine day, is it not?"

The guard's mouth curved as he lowered his eyes and took in the curves of her body.

With a languorous sigh, Mac looked back toward the merchants' stalls. "Will you have time later to…" She lifted soft eyes to his. "Sup?" She held his gaze with round, not-quite-innocent eyes.

He shifted his weight as his smoldering eyes swept down to her breasts. Mac took in a deep breath and let it out slowly, letting her breasts rise and lower along with her breathing. The guard reached out and trailed a finger down her jawline then strayed to her lips as the carts and foot traffic continued around them. A strong hand gripped Mac by the arm and yanked her away from the guard.

The guard stepped back immediately and met Hamish's anger with the calm authority that came with his job. "The lass did nothing wrong."

"Did she not?" Hamish's anger was mounting.

Mac turned pleading eyes to his. "I swear it. Why would I, my darlin'?" She put her hand on his chest and gave him a cajoling smile. "*Och*, darlin', you ken how I feel about you."

The guard smirked. "Are you coming or going? There're folks behind you."

Hamish gave Mac a mollified look and moved forward, leading the pony and cart with one hand and gripping her arm with the other. She cast a quick, petulant look at the guard and walked on through the gate and over the cobbled road that led away from the castle.

Ciarán pulled the tarp open enough to make a slit for fresh air and a view of Mac. "Are you all right?"

Still shaken by the events of the last half hour, Mac took a few halting breaths. "Better now." She continued to gulp breaths and then took hold of the edge of the cart.

Ciarán put his hand over hers. "Easy, lass. You'll get light-headed."

She nodded quickly but continued to draw deep, uneven breaths.

Hamish pulled off the road and into the cover of trees. He stopped and threw off the oilcloth. Ciarán climbed out of the cart and pulled Mac into his arms. She was gasping for air.

Words came in fits and starts as she caught her breath. "I haven't had this since I was a child. But I don't know. I guess the fear triggered it. I don't know."

Ciarán held onto her shoulders with sure hands, taking care not to interfere with her breathing. As a minute passed, and then another, her breathing grew even and calm.

She shook her head. "It's all right. I'm all right. We should go now. Where are the horses?"

Ciarán smiled helplessly. "Are you able to ride?"

"Yes."

"*Och*. Come here, bonnie Mac," he said as he pulled her into his arms. "You were very brave."

Mac lifted doubtful eyes to meet his. "If shaking with fear makes me brave."

Ciarán brushed a strand of Mac's hair from her face and gazed at her with soft eyes. "No, it does not, but shaking with fear and still doing what you did does make you brave."

Before she could respond, Ciarán kissed her.

Ciarán looked up as Hamish approached. With a sigh, Ciarán held Mac close, cradling her head in the crook of his neck.

Hamish said, "We must go. They may be after us yet."

Ciarán gave his brother a nod and sent him away with a look. Hamish did not look pleased, but he left them alone.

With a soft kiss on Mac's forehead, Ciarán said, "We'll finish this later." He slid his hand down her shoulder and arm and took hold of her hand to lead her to their horse. He helped her up onto the horse and then mounted behind her.

They rode until dusk and made camp upon a wooded brae. Hamish and Fergus hunted for supper, and Ciarán stayed behind with Mac. He set about building a fire in uncomfortable silence.

When he'd finished, Ciarán said without looking,

"Why have you come, lass?" His voice had lost its former warmth.

"You can't just say things like you said and then leave."

He glanced briefly at her with a look so stern that Mac was glad it was only a glance. Without turning from his fire building, he said, "It isnae safe for you here."

"From what I've seen, it isn't that safe for you either."

Ciarán stopped what he was doing and looked over at her. Mac met his gaze, although flinching would have been her first choice. His expression was hard enough without the evening shadows of swaying tree branches.

"You shouldnae have come. What if you had met up with ruffians?"

"Ruffians?" Mac started to laugh but caught herself. It still felt so unreal, as though she were in some sort of Renaissance fair gone wrong. She had to remind herself that she was actually in the eighteenth century. "Lucky thing I found Hamish and Fergus."

Ciarán folded his arms. "They found you. But you were, indeed, fortunate, lass. From now on, do not go anywhere without one of us."

His voice had an edge that matched a stern look Mac had not seen from him before. He had no right to take such an air of authority with her.

She lifted her chin in defiance. "I was close to the castle. I would have been fine."

"Would you now?" Ciarán turned and looked at her with a haunting expression. "You could have met with so many dangers that I dare not think on it."

"So could you. But you didn't, because I got you out. Or have you forgotten that part?" Mac took a breath. He had made a good point, but she would not let him know it.

"Hamish and Fergus would have gotten me out."

"Oh? Then why didn't they?"

Ciarán clenched his jaw as he looked into the woods. "That's a very good question, which I'll pose to them when they've returned. But now we are talking about you."

Mac stood up and brushed off her skirt. "I think we've covered that subject." She had tried to sound flippant, but she felt her emotions too close to the surface. She had never been able to hide feelings well. So she did what she always did; she walked away. At least this way she felt some semblance of control— that is, until she tripped on a tree root and fell. Her knee struck the root, and the pain spread through her body, jolting unfiltered emotions and a few choice curse words.

"Where does it hurt?" Ciarán asked in gentle, sure tones as he knelt down beside her.

My heart. That was what she wanted to tell him, but instead she said, "My knee."

He put both hands around her ankle and worked his way up, checking for broken bones.

Mac said softly, "I may have hurt my other knee, too."

"Oh, aye?" His voice had lost most of its harshness. She could see that he wanted to smile, but he fought it. Instead, he called her bluff and examined the other leg.

When he got to her knee, Mac took in a breath. His strong fingers were electric. Neither one of them moved.

"We've got supper," Fergus called out as he emerged from the woods, toting a duck and a rabbit.

Ciarán slipped his hand away and helped Mac to her feet. With a firm hand on her upper arm, he led her back to the fire. When he started to support her so she could sit down, she said, "It's better now, thank you." She gently but deliberately eased her arm from his grasp.

While the supper was cooking over the fire, Ciarán said, "Hamish, would you care to tell me how it came to be that you let a woman do what you should have done?" The edge in his voice cut through the restless air stirring between them.

Hamish took a long moment before responding. "The lass had a good idea."

Ciarán said, "One that put her in danger."

"We were always nearby in case anything happened," said Fergus.

"Nearby? Outside the castle?" Ciarán's voice remained quiet but grew more intense.

"Aye," Fergus said firmly.

"Could you not bring a ransom?" Ciarán tossed a broken tree branch on the fire. Sparks floated into the night sky.

Hamish started to grin. "I did, but why waste a good ransom?"

In one move, Ciarán leapt toward Hamish and hurled him backward onto the ground. Hamish wriggled free and struck Ciarán, who in turn landed a blow on Hamish's jaw that sent him back once more to the ground. In an instant, he was up with his hands around Ciarán's neck. They rolled around for a bit until Fergus strode over and pulled them apart. "That's enough, lads."

Ciarán glared at Hamish. "If you ever put her life at risk again, I'll put yours at risk, too—and you too, Fergus." Ciarán turned and walked away, muttering something about getting more wood for the fire.

Hamish frowned as he brushed himself off. "Watch him, lass. Your sweetheart has a temper." His eyes sparkled with amusement.

"My sweetheart?" In light of all that had happened, Mac was not sure how to react. She and

Ciarán had barely spoken, and although he had kissed her, "sweetheart" was a bit of a leap from where they were right now.

Hamish gave her his most charming grin, and it made Mac uneasy. She looked away to avoid his knowing look. She would not let him see he was right.

Having vented their anger, the men settled around the fire to quietly share a flask of whisky while Mac tried to work through her competing emotions. She had arrived with one purpose in mind: to find Ciarán, which she had done. After that, she had thought only of rescuing him, which she also had done. But now, here she was with her mission accomplished, and she felt completely off-balance. What had she expected? And what did she want? She had done something drastic: traveled through time on the strength of one heart-pounding kiss, and for what? What did she think would—or could—happen now? Yes, there was an attraction. She could not deny it. But this was not some sort of spring-break romance. Nor was it real life—at least not hers. This was more like a dream from which she would awaken, having lost something that she had never really had.

Fergus interrupted her thoughts. "We'd best sleep, aye?"

The other two men uttered grunts of agreement as they rose and went to their horses to get blankets for sleeping. Ciarán returned with a spare plaid, which he held out to Mac.

"No, thank you." Pride had prompted her answer, but a cold gust of wind soon made her regret it.

"Dinnae be a fool."

As if she had not heard him, Mac wrapped herself in her lightweight woolen tartan and lay down on the cold ground. She dozed off a few times, only to awaken to her own shivers and Fergus's snores. With the moon high in the sky, morning had to be hours off. She was in the midst of longing for the down duvet from her bed at home when a warm plaid was draped over her and a large and very warm body drew close behind her and cradled her in its warmth.

Mac opened her eyes wide.

"Dinnae argue with me, woman. I'll not have you freeze," Ciarán said in a low voice close to her ear as he wrapped his arm around her waist and pulled her against him. She sank into his warmth and breathed in his scent. She soon drifted off to sleep in his arms.

11

A PROMISE FULFILLED

WHEN SHE AWOKE in the morning, Ciarán was gone. Hamish and Fergus were eating.

Fergus handed her a cup. "Hurry and break your fast. We'll be leaving soon."

As she sat down on her tartan to eat, Mac eyed the watery porridge with suspicion. "On the bright side, there's no way I won't lose a pound or two while I'm here."

Hamish and Fergus started saddling their horses. Ciarán's horse was there, but there was still no sign of Ciarán. Fergus glanced over, which she took as a sign that they were waiting for her, but with limited patience. She gulped the last bit of porridge and stood up. A strong hand gripped her arm and pulled her up the rest of the way to the horse.

"Make haste," Ciarán said. "A small party from Clan Ross is headed our way."

"Where are we going?" Mac asked as Ciarán pulled her up to ride behind him.

"Away," Ciarán answered. "Hold tight, Mac." And with that, they were off.

The terrain was rocky and rough. Climbing as fast as they did spoke well of Ciarán's skill as a horseman and of his horse's speed. Even so, they could not keep up with Hamish and Fergus, whose horses had only one rider to carry. Hamish doubled back to ride beside them. "We cannae outride them at this pace."

"No." Ciarán shared a knowing look with Hamish, who nodded.

"The caves, then?" asked Hamish.

Ciarán stared into the distance. "Aye."

With a nod, Hamish urged his horse on as they headed into a pass between two hills.

The cave was well hidden behind jutting rocks. Although the entrance was narrow and deep, after a few minutes they turned into a larger chamber that had a fissure which allowed sunlight in from high above. There was room for them here, horses and all.

Mac asked Ciarán, "How long will we wait here?"

"Until we're safe to go home," Ciarán said as though that were enough of an answer.

Mac tried to keep her voice patient. "And when will that be?"

Ciarán turned to her. "I dinnae ken. It depends upon them. If they ride past us, we'll need to wait for them to turn back and go home. If they follow our trail, we'll fight them."

"Here?"

"Aye."

For Ciarán, this was a simple decision that he took in stride, but for Mac, the reality of it was harsh. Violence was a part of life here. People grew up with it, prepared for it, and accepted its consequences. But Mac knew nothing about how to survive in this world.

After being lost in thought for several moments, Mac glanced up to find Ciarán studying her. It would have been a good moment for him to tell her that everything would be fine and that he would keep her safe. But try though he would, even great warriors fell. If he did, she would be helpless, and she knew it.

Without a word, he took her hand and led her around the bend in the cave. There, he handed a *sgian dubh* to her. "'Tis a small weapon, but effective up close." He showed her how to best hold and wield it. "Dinnae hesitate. Strike to kill, for you'll not have a second chance."

Mac gave a determined nod and slipped the knife under her belt, but her trembling hand betrayed her. Ciarán put his sure hand over hers and lifted it. Gently, he brushed his lips over her fingers. "You have yet to answer my question. Why have you come here?"

"You told me that I would love you."

"Aye, but you didnae know me then."

"No, but I thought that I might."

"Know me?" His searching eyes stirred her soul.

"Love you." Mac had never felt so exposed. Instinct told her to turn away, but she could not take her eyes from his. "The way that you said it made me wish it were true."

A gentle smile warmed his eyes. "And what else did I tell you?"

"That you would love me," she whispered.

He brushed a wisp of hair from her brow and smiled gently. "Ah, but you see, I already did."

"And now?"

"And now." He cupped the back of her head in his hand and drew her into a kiss.

The nearby voices of Hamish and Fergus reminded them that they were not alone. Ciarán leaned back in an effort to put a safe distance between them, but it only served to afford him a view of the slope of her neck to her shoulders and breasts, which his hands further explored. But he stopped, put his hands on her shoulders, and let out a guttural sigh. "My lovely Mac, I believe you have come to torment me."

She smiled, and his answering smile filled her with

joy. "Not being with you like this was my torment. That's why I went through the stone chamber."

Ciarán grinned. "So you could watch me go mad from wanting you?" He laughed as he lifted and spun her around. But their laughter soon faded as he slid her body down against his and set her feet on the ground. They clung together. His breath warmed her neck as he whispered, "I am yours, Mistress Mackenzie."

Fergus cleared his throat loudly and walked past them on his way outside. "I'll keep the first watch."

Ciarán exchanged somber looks with Fergus. "Good. I'll relieve you when night falls."

Mac saw the concern in his eyes as he watched Fergus leave. He was thinking of what was to come. If the Clan Ross men found them, they would be outnumbered. The very thing that now kept them protected could become their downfall, for if discovered, they would be trapped in the cave with no means of escape. But it was their best option now.

Ciarán turned back to Mac. "We must rest while we're able." He touched her back gently, and they went into the back of the cave. There was no fire, lest it give them away. Ciarán lay beside Mac and warmed her until she fell asleep, then he quietly went outside to join Fergus. Hamish followed.

Fergus said, "Before darkness fell, I caught a glimpse of some smoke at the foot of the mountain."

Hamish scratched his chin as he considered this. "We're a day's ride away, and they've a climb ahead of them if they're coming up here."

"'Tis true," Ciarán said. "But if they go around the mountain, we might meet them on the other side."

Fergus shook his head. "A good tracker could find our trail. There's a good chance they will follow it up here to us."

Hamish nodded. "Aye, but we've a downhill path before us. We have the advantage."

Ciarán ran his hand through his hair and exhaled. "Either we take the downhill path and risk meeting Clan Ross or wait in the cave while they pass by. Waiting would be the safer option." They all knew he was thinking of Mac, but no one voiced it.

It was Fergus who broke the silence. "Unless they know of the cave—then we'd be trapped."

It was a point no one could argue with.

"'Tis your lady at risk. What say you, Ciarán?" Hamish asked.

Ciarán knew they would defer to him, for if he chose their course and anything happened to her, he would not be able to blame them. It would be his own fault, so he considered his options with care. "We leave at dawn."

A THUNDER OF HORSES

AT DAWN, they rode the path down the mountain. Now on relatively level ground, they looked forward to half a day's ride, but first they stopped by a burn to water the horses. Mac knelt by the water, splashed her face, and brushed her teeth with the travel toothbrush she'd brought as a small self-indulgence. Now more alert thanks to the ice-cold water, she tucked her toothbrush back into her pocket. She smiled to herself. All she needed now was for David to arrive on his bike with a fresh cup of coffee in hand.

The sound of thundering horses jarred her back to the present. She looked up to see Ciarán running to her. He threw her onto the horse and leapt up behind her. The others were already mounted. Off they rode with half a dozen Rosses behind them.

"Get down, love, and hold onto the mane!" Ciarán shouted in her ear.

As flintlock rifles fired, Ciarán leaned over Mac to protect her. Her heart swelled with deep affection that she dared not call love, but along with it came fear. She could lose him this day. All she could do was revel in the strength of his body against hers and the heart she was drawn to.

They were riding fine horses that, so far, had kept pace ahead of the Rosses, but Ciarán and Mac's horse had two people to carry. "There's a good lad," said Ciarán as he urged his horse onward. "Mac, do you have your *sgian dubh*?"

"Yes."

"Keep your hand on it, lass."

Eilean Donan Castle was faint in the distance, but the Rosses drew closer. Ciarán stopped his horse by a boulder. In one swift motion, he pulled Mac from the horse and set her down on the ground. The movement was so sudden that it nearly knocked the wind out of her.

"Take this pistol. It's loaded," Ciarán said. "Hide behind that boulder."

"No! Take me with you. I'll fight. Let me help you!"

Without acknowledging her pleas, Ciarán turned and headed straight for the Rosses. He stood shoulder to shoulder with Hamish and Fergus.

"Halt!" Hamish called to the other men. "You're on Eilean Donan land now."

Six men from Clan Ross stopped to face them. Their pistols and rifles were drawn. "Ciarán MacRae, come with us," one of them ordered.

"'Tis a fool's mission you're on," Ciarán said. "Did you really think they would pay a ransom for me? Have they yet? Even if you can take me, I'm no use to you."

The one in charge said, "I'll agree that you're useless, but now 'tis a matter of pride."

Hamish said, "Turn around and go home. There's nothing here for you."

With his pistol aimed at Ciarán, the leader said, "Oh, but there is. There's the matter of a ransom."

Hamish laughed. "We havenae got it. Do you not think we'd have paid it by now?"

The leader grinned as he saw Mac walking toward them. "Well, she's no ransom, but she'll do for a start."

Ciarán muttered a curse. From inside the folds of her skirt, Mac drew a pistol. Two men from the Ross party turned their rifles toward her. She surprised everyone by directing her pistol at Ciarán's brother. With a narrowed eyes, she said, "Hamish is going to give you the ransom. In turn, you'll ride away, and our business is settled. Are we agreed?"

The leader grinned. "Aye, wench, we're agreed.

'Tis a shame we can't stay and acquaint ourselves better. Perhaps another day."

In even tones, Ciarán said, "Touch her and I'll kill you." His direct look drew an uncomfortable smile from the Ross leader.

"Hamish." Mac took a step closer. "Give the men their ransom." She watched Hamish consider his options, which she had thought through already. He could refuse her orders. Perhaps she would not have the courage to shoot him, but if she faltered, the Rosses would oblige. Ciarán and Fergus would put up a fight, which they might win. Even so, with everyone focused on him at the moment, Hamish's chances looked worst of all.

"God's teeth, woman!" As he scowled, the sharp look in his eyes sent a shiver through Mac. "You'll pay for this."

His words prompted a warning grunt from Ciarán, which Hamish seemed to understand. Hamish's face showed the strain as he lifted his hands and said, "I'm going to lower my pistol."

"No, give it over." One of the Rosses approached and took the pistol from Hamish. He handed it off to another man.

"Dismount," said the leader.

When Hamish hesitated, Fergus said, "You'd best do as he says."

"As should you all," said another Ross.

After they all dismounted, the leader ordered his men to search each of them. "The wench included."

As one man took her pistol and leered, Mac said, "Try anything, pal, and I'll knee you so hard that you'll have to crawl home."

He laughed and began searching her, starting with her ankles. When he reached the top of her thighs, she jabbed the *sgian dubh* into his hand. "That's off limits."

He grabbed her wrist and wrenched the knife from it, then he pulled his hand back and struck her. Fergus held Ciarán back.

"That's enough," said the one in charge. He turned to Mac. "You had that coming." He chuckled. With the searching done, the Clan Ross men stowed the weapons, took the MacRae horses in tow, and rode off, leaving them standing in the glen.

When she felt they were a safe enough distance away, Mac looked over at Ciarán. He watched, jaw clenched, as the men rode away.

Mac said, "Thank God no one was hurt."

"Shut your damn gob, woman!" said Hamish.

While she had not expected Hamish to part easily with the ransom, she thought he would at least appreciate her having spared his brother another kidnapping. She looked to Ciarán, expecting something other than what she received, which was a cold glance before he turned away and started to walk toward the castle. Hamish followed. It was Fergus who came to her and said, "Come, lass. We've a long walk ahead."

They walked in silence for what must have been more than an hour. Mac's spirit sank further with each step. Ciarán had not said a word to her. Under his quiet demeanor, a fierce anger burned. When she could take no more, Mac asked, "Fergus, what did I do?"

He scoffed. "*Och.*"

Mac stared for a moment, sure that he would follow up with something. He did not.

"Oh, well, that explains it," she said sarcastically.

A full minute later, Fergus said, "You may as well cut off his balls, for all that you've done."

His words felt like a punch in the gut. When she could speak, Mac said, "Really?"

Fergus walked on in silence.

Mac shook her head. "That's what this is about?"

Fergus's head tilted just barely enough to register that he'd heard her.

"Oh, c'mon. If a man had done that, you'd be buying rounds at the pub and slapping each other's backs."

Fergus stopped in his tracks. "If a man had done that?" He looked at her directly.

"Yes!"

Fergus's eyes bore through her. "A man should have done that."

As Fergus resumed walking, Mac nodded. "Go on. I'll catch up."

They were near the stone chamber she had emerged from days ago. She glanced toward the others. They walked on, untroubled by her. So Mac turned and walked away, toward the chamber. She was caught up in her inner dialogue, vacillating between cursing men for their pride and berating herself for expecting them to appreciate modern sensibilities. Somewhere in the midst of her turmoil, she heard Ciarán calling her name. She saw no point in answering him, but she could not help but take one last look back to remember him by.

"Where are you going?" he called.

"Good-bye, Ciarán."

He was running toward her. Mac could not bear the thought of breaking down in front of him. As much as it hurt to admit it, they were too far apart. Time was the least of their problems. Both were strong-minded and rooted in opposing ways of life. Back home, she had thought that not knowing was the worst part of it all. She had made a mistake. Now she knew. She had traded longing for grief, for her heart would now break. All she wanted to do was go home and cry unobserved, but instead, she felt as though pieces of pride and self-esteem were sloughing off as she ran for the cave. No longer caring who heard her, she sputtered, "Who wants to live in a place that doesn't have pints of ice cream to cry over?" She started to stumble on a loose rock but recovered. "And I miss my hiking shoes, dammit!"

"Mac!"

"I'm fine! Just let me go!" Not bad, she thought. Her voice sounded more confident than she had expected it to.

He grabbed hold of her arm. Mac noted that Ciarán was breathing deeply but not gulping for air as she was. She made a mental note to crank up the incline on her treadmill. But for what? The next time she decided to break up with a guy while running uphill in Scotland?

"Mac, wait."

"Look, Ciarán, it's not me; it's you. Turns out it sucks to be a woman in the eighteenth-century High-lands. I get it. It'll take about 250 years before you'll be able to appreciate what I did for you. Until then, I'd just like to go home. Ring me up when you've evolved." She turned and walked away from him, feeling empowered but lonely for Ciarán already.

"The stone chamber's that way."

Mac stopped and shut her eyes for an instant. With a sigh, she turned and looked at him. He looked genuinely sorry for having to correct her.

Sheepishly, she asked, "Which way?"

He tilted his head back the other way. He could

have made fun of her—laughed, or at the very least, smirked. But he did not.

She gave him one point for that but then deducted it when his gaze settled on hers and made her heart melt just a little. Tears stung her eyes as she tried to suppress them. "Well, thank you. I guess I'll just, uh, be on my way."

As she walked past him, he grabbed her and planted the sort of kiss on her that she could not refuse.

"Oh c'mon! Would you stop doing that?" Her knees wanted to buckle, but she blamed it on the walking.

The corner of his mouth turned up as he said, "Stop doing what?" And he kissed her again.

When he finally released her, Mac awkwardly nodded while she searched for words. "Well, nobody said you couldn't kiss." She glanced up. He was smiling. Against her will, she smiled back. But her smile faded as the truth of the day's events weighed on her. "But it's not enough." She had to go now before she lost her composure. She took one step away and then turned back. "Just one more." And she took his face in her hands and kissed him. She took her time. There was touching involved.

With a gasp, she pulled back. "Good-bye."

Ciarán held her in a vise of an embrace. "I was

angry. I felt like a fool. Worse, you made us look like fools in front of our enemies."

"I know. I mean, I can see that now. But at the time, I was just trying to help you. They were going to hurt you—or worse—and I couldn't just stand there and watch."

He nodded.

"Hamish could have just given them the money, but he didn't." She stopped short of saying that Hamish had chosen the money over Ciarán, but he had to know that already. To say it would only hurt him more. "The truth is, if a man had done what I did, you would not have been angry."

He nodded again. "'Tis true. I'd have been angry with Hamish. God's teeth, the man likes a good bargain. He wouldnae part with a milk cow to save me."

"And I made him part with gold."

Ciarán shrugged. "Aye, so he lost a bargain this time. He'll recover."

Mac shook her head slowly. "It's so different here."

His eyes met hers and made her heart ache. "Too different."

She looked down at his leine and touched the coarse fabric. "I should go home now."

He lifted his brows with helpless resignation. "'Tis too late. There's not enough light."

Mac's spirits sank. She had been ready to make a clean break. She could not start to get over him until she could be free of his soft eyes, strong jaw, and full lips—and the arms that held her against him so her head lay on his chest, where his scent made her want to swoon.

Ciarán said, "And I dinnae want you to go."

She shook her head. "I'm bound to make you angry again."

"Aye." His warm smile was infectious.

"I don't fit in here."

He had no charming reaction to this. The truth that Mac could not bring herself to admit aloud was that she never would fit in. Nor could she. She had never intended to stay here. The fact that she was even thinking about it scared her.

"We have different ways, but you can learn to understand them," Ciarán said.

Mac could not deny that he'd made a good point. He was willing to meet her halfway, which was more than she imagined his brother would do—or anyone else here. Even if Ciarán could accept her, others would not. As much as she wished it could be, it could not.

Mac said softly, "What's the point?"

He lifted her chin and looked into her soul. "You are."

She gazed back, a helpless victim of her heart, for

she ached to be with him. "I'll have to go back at some point."

"Not today, or tomorrow." He said it like a command.

"No, not until after my heart breaks completely."

He took her with fierce desperation into his arms and kissed her with a force that made her head swim. They could not get close enough, pressing and clutching. She gripped his belt, pulling him closer.

With breathless impatience, Mac said, "Where are Hamish and Fergus? They'll see us."

"I told them to go home without us."

"Good." She clutched at his kilt, lifting it out of her way.

"No." Ciarán gripped her shoulders and pushed her to arm's length. "I'll not take you like this."

"It's okay," Mac assured him.

But Ciarán would not be swayed. "No. It would not be right."

Mac tried to form a question, but she could not find an argument for this.

Gently, he kissed her. Her whole body went liquid.

"Keep that up, Scotty, and my head will explode —and my ovaries, too."

Confused by her remark, he shook his head slowly and grinned. "Lovely lassie, I have never known anyone like you."

She frowned. "Yeah, I get that a lot—but not in a good way."

He held out his hand. "Will you come home with me now?"

"For now," she said, slipping her hand into his. Even as the warmth of his strong hand against hers made the blood rush to her cheeks, she knew she was making a mistake.

13

THE HOMECOMING

CIARÁN TOOK the oars and rowed the boat to the castle while Mac sat, untroubled for the first time since she had arrived. But as she watched Ciarán row, with his arm muscles flexing, a new trouble took over. He was simply a fine man to look at. Strong body, sure mind, and a smile that made her want to lift her chin to it as though it were the sun.

He smiled curiously at her. "What's on your mind, lass?"

Suppressing her own smile, she said, "Nothing."

He stopped rowing and leaned his elbows on his knees. "Oh, I think not, my fair maiden. 'Twas something. Your face was fair glowing."

A blush spread through her cheeks, but something about his self-assurance made her want to conceal it. "You don't have to know all that I'm thinking."

"But I want to." He lifted his eyes to meet hers with a gaze so direct that her heart leapt to her throat. "I want to ken every part of your mind and your body." He reached out for her hand, and she gave it to him. He slid his fingertip up one of her fingers and down the next as he said, "Every nook, every cranny, every hidden part that no one else sees or touches, I want to make mine." When she did not look at him, he took her face in his hands. "Mac." And he tilted her face so she had to look at him. He said simply, "I love you." Not waiting for her reaction, he kissed her.

Mac sank into his arms, gripping his shirt fabric as though she might drown. There was no help for her now. From this point on, her heart would ache in his absence.

Sensing her apprehension, Ciarán looked at her calmly and said, "I will be by your side, and I will keep you safe."

Mac knew that he meant it, but she knew he could not keep her heart safe—not from him or from her own flood of emotions. Common sense told her to flee, but she stayed and said nothing. And by failing to voice her true feelings, she set a new course. She could no longer convince herself that this feeling was anything other than love, for she knew that it was. And this love was the sort that would last, even though she would soon have to leave him. Still clutching his shirt, she pulled him close and kissed him. She wanted him now with no thought but to touch him and taste him until it was time for her to leave. He held her and answered her longing with his. And that was when she was sure that both their hearts would break.

WHEN THEY ARRIVED at the castle, the celebration had already begun. Hamish and Fergus had already arrived. A great feast and much ale and whisky were provided for all to share in the celebration of Ciarán's release from captivity. Hamish did not directly claim credit, but neither he nor Fergus discouraged people from forming such a conclusion.

Clasping Mac's hand, Ciarán kept her in tow for a time until whisky and manly pats on the back and embraces swept him away. He looked back once or twice, but Mac just grinned and waved as someone new would draw him into more talking and laughter.

Perhaps if there had been a woman to talk to, to pull her aside and draw her into a circle of friends, she might have felt more at home. But there was none. All the women here were either working or scattered about in small groups, heads together in close conversation. None of them invited her to join them, so Mac wandered around largely unnoticed. They had seen her with Ciarán, so they knew she belonged in the sense that she was not a threat, for no one belonged there less than she. Even so, she reminded herself that this was a rare opportunity to observe life in these turbulent times in history. Flames from the fire and wall sconces cast a soft light on the people whose faces were lined not only with the harshness of life but also with laughter. There was a sense of community that had been lost in the generations that led to her lifetime.

She glanced over at Ciarán and smiled. He was having a grand time. He was clearly well-liked and as happy with his friends as they were with him. He was rooted in the history of his clan and held up by the loyal clansmen around him as much as they were by him. They were strong and secure as a people and as individual men and women who were parts of something much greater. And Ciarán was one of them, inextricably bound to life here. This was something that Mac loved about him, but it would be their undoing. For as much as he was part of his life here, so she was anchored to her own life—to her sister. Without Cam, she would feel adrift, as would Cam without her. It was one more reminder of why she could not stay.

Someone handed her a cup of whisky, which she drank, and another, which she also drank. At some point, Ciarán was swept away, and she lost track of him. Guests made their way to long tables set up in the great hall for supper. A young woman handed her baby to an older woman beside her and took her place beside a small group of musicians. While the fiddle, lute, and bodhrán played, the young woman sang with a tone that was clear and pure. Mac was transfixed.

A firm hand grasped hers. Without looking, she knew him. His touch sent a surge of energy passing between them.

"Bonnie lass, would you join me for supper?"

A smile formed unbidden from her heart, and it shone through her eyes as she looked at him. "Why, yes, sir, I would."

He grinned and led her between the two long rows of tables lining the walls until they arrived at the dais. There they sat at the high table beside Hamish, the constable of the castle. Although Clan MacKenzie owned Eilean Donan, the MacRaes were entrusted with keeping it for them. Mac did not need to wonder what Ciarán's role was in the castle. Although he was clearly liked and respected, he held no formal title. Any function he had in the workings here was of Hamish's granting. Hamish respected his brother and sought his advice. Mac suspected they had fought side by side. Although Ciarán showed no signs of it bothering him, Mac had to wonder if it sometimes irked him to be at Hamish's mercy solely because of birth order. But as the thought came, she dismissed it. She thought of her sister and how it would be if they had to share power. There would be the usual squabbles, but they would rise above it. It must be so with Ciarán and Hamish.

While the meal was served, a series of toasts began, the first one being to Ciarán. Hamish welcomed him home, and a rumble of echoing sentiments followed.

Ciarán stood and quieted them. "I am here by the grace of my brother and this lovely lass by my side. She goes by the name of Mac. Although I find her name passing strange, I find the lady, herself, passing fair." A low rumble of agreement rose from the tables. "And I ask that you welcome her here." With that, he lifted her hand and bent down to kiss it. With a boyish grin, he lifted his eyes and gave her a wink. Turning back to the guests, he said, "Celebrate my good fortune, my friends, for I will, I assure you!" People laughed and returned to their own drinks and conversations.

She caught ribald remarks and crude glances from those at a table nearby. Diverting her glances only brought other similar looks. "Ciarán." She turned to him and said his name again. When he turned, she said under her breath, "People think you're going to 'celebrate' me."

He glanced at her air quotes with a now-familiar look of confusion. It always passed quickly, for he seemed to have learned to dismiss such things as small signs of her strange, modern ways.

Mac tried again. "They think I'm your round-heeled wench."

After a moment of thought, he grinned, having understood her meaning.

Mac met his grin with narrowing eyes. "I did not travel back in time just to boink you."

He started to laugh, for her meaning was clear, but the hurt look in her eyes stopped him. He looked somberly at her. "Why did you come back?" he asked as if he knew the answer.

Mac looked down at her food. She would not make a scene. Softly, she said, "I don't know. I was curious to know what you'd be like."

He cocked his head slightly. "To boink?" He let his grin spread to his eyes and watched for her reaction. He leaned closer and whispered. "There it is."

"There what is?"

"The color in your cheeks." He brushed one of her cheeks with his knuckles. "If dozens of eyes were not watching, I'd kiss you here, and down here on each patch of color."

With a glance toward the tables of people that lined the great hall, Mac took hold of his hand and gently pulled it from her neck. "Please stop. You're embarrassing me."

He drew back, plainly confused, but he acquiesced

with a nod. "As you wish." He then turned away and proceeded to busy himself drinking whisky and talking to Hamish. For the rest of the evening, he made no further effort to talk, let alone touch.

More music followed dinner. This was livelier. The crowd spilled out to the bailey. For the first time in more than an hour, Ciarán rose and left her sitting alone. Hamish was turned away, talking. Mac felt ill at ease, so she rose and, with no place else to go, went out to the bailey. Amid all the merriment, she was lonely. A few women greeted her with shy respect. Men went out of their way to avoid her, no doubt out of respect for Ciarán. If she had been told where her room was, she would have gone to it now. She was exhausted. The one place she knew in a castle was the kitchen. Even if they saw her as Ciarán's wench, they would not dare turn her away. So she went there and sought out a corner near the fire where she could curl up and rest.

The activity calmed down around her as the kitchen work was completed and the hour grew late. Mac drifted to sleep, sitting on the floor, leaning against the stone wall. As she dozed, she heard the distant scuffle of feet but then drifted into a deep sleep.

After the fire had grown cold, powerful arms lifted her. Mac awoke. She breathed in his scent and knew without looking that it was Ciarán. But she did look up at him. "I fell asleep."

"So I gathered."

"I'm awake now. I can walk." After she said it, she wished she had not, for his arms were so warm.

Ciarán set her down and took her hand to lead her through the castle and up a narrow spiral flight of stairs. They stopped in front of a door, which he unlocked and gently pushed open. Embers glowed in the fireplace, casting a warm glow on the foot of a bed thick with linens and blankets.

"Sleep here."

"Where will you be?"

"I'll be nearby."

"Where?"

"Across the hall."

The way he said it made it sound far away. But he was close now, and she wanted to feel his arms on her and his body against hers.

Ciarán gestured for her to enter. "Go on. Get some rest."

She passed the threshold but then turned and put a hand on his arm. "Ciarán, wait. I'm sorry. I know that you're angry. But I felt uncomfortable. People were leering as though I were—"

"I ken what you thought." His anger cut through the air between them as he lifted her hand and set it carefully down to hang at her side. "Go in. Latch the door."

Mac glanced at the door, hoping door locks had not changed in the past three hundred years.

Seeing the look on her face, Ciarán opened the door and stepped inside her room. With a hint of impatience, he showed her the latch. "Here. Close the door and then slide your thumb so, and 'tis latched." He took a step back but stopped short of leaving the room.

Masked in shadows, they looked at each other, feeling more than they saw in the dark of the tension between them. Mac opened her mouth to speak, but words did not come easily. Ciarán shifted his weight, and she feared he would leave.

"Ciarán, I'm sorry."

"Are you?"

Mac started to reach out, but he undid the latch and started to leave her room.

"Yes." She withdrew her hand. "I just felt—I don't know. I'm not used to a lot of attention and the way they were staring."

"Aye, 'tis true. They were staring. And you thought the worst—of them and of me." He walked into the hallway toward his room but stopped and turned back.

Mac stood in her doorway. "They were leering," she said. "It was no reflection on you."

"No reflection?" Deliberately dispassionate eyes met hers. "Because I am a barbarous man who puts his women on display for the rabble to ogle?"

"I never said that. I just felt uncomfortable."

"Aye, 'tis no wonder."

Mac was not sure what he meant by that, but she did not have to wait long to find out.

Ciarán said, "I'll not argue that your ways are not different from ours, but I'll not agree that they're better. For what good is it if you're so caught up in yourself that you cannae see what's before you?"

Mac bristled. "Well, I don't appreciate that."

"You don't like it, you mean, because it's true."

Mac gasped as her temper flared. "I just don't like people staring. If that makes me caught up in myself, you're no better."

"Oh, aye?"

"Aye—I mean, yes! You put me on display like a trophy to puff up your ego."

"My what?"

"Never mind!" Only then did she lower her eyes, but she could not get past his full lips. They were now inches from hers.

Ciarán fell as silent as she, except for their breathing. Mac leaned away, but it was not enough, so she took a step backward.

The light from the wall sconce flickered across Ciarán's muscular arms as he gripped the doorframe and leaned closer. In a voice so controlled that it was chilling, he said, "If anyone stared, it was because no woman has sat by my side at that table before." Mac's eyes widened even as Ciarán's narrowed. "They were happy to see it for my sake. So dinnae judge my people harshly for being different from yours. They love me, as I love them. And they would have loved you."

He glanced down as he quietly closed the door between them. Mac stared at the door until the echo of Ciarán's own closing door faded to nothing.

14

THE PROPER ORDER OF THINGS

A SERIES of raps at the door woke Mac. She had hoped to hear Ciarán's voice, but it was only a chambermaid. She set down a tray with porridge and ale and then added some wood to the fire. Mac asked if she might have a bath. The maid left and returned with an armful of clothing and a series of servants in tow carrying a wooden bath tub and pails of steaming hot water. When they offered to stay to assist, Mac thanked them and insisted that she would manage from there.

She did not. The bathing was as close to luxurious as one could get in these times, but dressing was another thing altogether. She had thought her college summers working at a Renaissance fair would equip her for the task, but, although she had a fairly good idea of what went on and in what order, she wound up with some leftover pieces. When she'd lost patience with the whole operation, she called down the stairs to the guard to please fetch her chambermaid.

The servant breezed in and took one look at Mac. "Oh, miss!" She politely averted her eyes and caught sight of one of the spare pieces of fabric. "Do they not wear pockets where you're from?"

"I'm afraid not—at least not quite like this."

Without hesitation, the chambermaid set about relacing, tying, and putting things right. Paying close attention as the servant tied on the pockets and skirt, Mac said, "So that's where those things go!"

The young woman looked at her, trying to discreetly suppress a giggle, but it burst forth as their eyes met and Mac laughed with her. "They're pockets, mistress. Your skirts open here on the sides so you can reach in."

Mac's face lit up. "Oh! Well, that makes perfect sense, doesn't it?"

With a broad smile, the young woman said, "Aye." She adjusted Mac's kerchief. "There, miss. How bonnie you look!"

"Thank you…what's your name?"

"Janet, miss." After a quick smile and curtsey, she gathered up Mac's clothes.

Mac reached out. "No. Leave them, please."

Janet looked puzzled. "Do you not wish me to wash them?"

"No, thank you. Just leave them on the chair."

With a hint of disapproval that she quickly shook off, Janet complied and left with a cheery good-bye.

As the door closed behind Janet, Mac said to herself, "The last thing they need is to get a look at a zipper. Their heads would explode." She then tore her repurposed bridesmaid's dress at the seams and fed it piece by piece to the fire, followed closely by her bra. She could not help but think that her feminist mother would have been proud to see her daughter tossing her bra to the flames.

MAC MADE her way downstairs with an eye out for Ciarán. Having no luck, she went outside, muttering, "He can't have gone far; the place is surrounded by water."

She was met with cordial greetings wherever she went, but she saw no sign of Ciarán. Finally, after having nearly circled the whole island, she heard splashing and saw what looked like Ciarán swimming toward the shore. She drew closer to be sure. He stood in the waist-deep water and started walking to the shore. It was Ciarán. Until now, Mac had not thought about what Highlanders wore to go swimming. Apparently nothing. He walked to a rumpled pile of plaid, which Mac only now noticed. His sword and targe were nearby, although how

she managed to look away long enough to ascertain that
was a wonder. Her gaze was helplessly fixed. It looked as
though he had come here straight from training and had
dropped everything on his way into the water. She might
have enjoyed the sight more if their last words had not
been spoken in anger. Instead, she could only manage to
stare at the man whom she feared she had lost.

Mac had never considered herself the sort to ogle
naked men, but for Ciarán, she made an exception.
Evidently, she could be swayed by broad shoulders,
solid abs, muscled thighs, and, well, yes—there was
that.

"Were you looking for something?" He looked
plainly at her, but behind his otherwise neutral facade,
his eyes smoldered from their exchange of words the
night before.

The sound of his voice was startling enough, but
to look up and see him watching her watch him unsettled her further. She turned away and shut her eyes
for a moment. "Sorry. I didn't know you were…well I
did, but I didn't mean to stare." Her voice trailed off
to a whisper. "Shut up, Mac."

He shrugged his leine on over his shoulders and
then scooped up his plaid and the rest. He took a
moment before moving to join her. "Were you looking
for me?"

She flinched. His approach had been silent. "Who

else would I look for? I'm sorry. I didn't mean to sound—" She exhaled. "Look, I just wanted to tell you I'm sorry."

When he said nothing, Mac's heart sank, but she rattled on, fearing the silence. "Look, I realize now that I jumped to conclusions. I was uneasy, and it clouded my thinking. But in my defense, going back three hundred years is not exactly easy. Truth be told, it's not like you see in the movies." She flinched yet again when he touched her. His hands were heavy and warm on her shoulders.

His jaw clenched then relaxed. "I've been thinking."

"Oh God." She did not mean to say the words, but they came out nonetheless. What did it matter now? He was going to send her away.

He turned her around by the shoulders to face him. Bitter embers still darkened his gaze. "'Tis a frightening thing to travel to another time."

"It wasn't fear, although God knows I've felt plenty of that here."

"Then what was it?" There was a gentle tone in his voice now that made her heart ache.

She lifted her eyes to his and shook her head. "I spent most of the night trying to figure it out. The same thing could have happened in my time, but there I've got other things in my life that are mine.

Here, I've got nothing. I don't fit in, and it made me feel very alone."

He pulled her against him, holding her head to his chest. "You are not alone." He said it so adamantly that she thought she might melt into him. When she lost her parents, her sense of balance had wavered, but her sister had been there as an anchor. Now Ciarán gave her that same sort of feeling. He was solid, and she felt secure. At the same time, she did not want to need him like that, for then she would have to trust him—a feeling that did not come easily to her. She was unsure of whether she ever would trust him enough—or any man, for that matter— to give him her heart. But she could not tell him that.

He kissed her hair. "I should have prepared you."

"How could you have?"

"I dinnae ken. Even so, I should never have left you alone."

Mac tilted her face up to his. "I can take care of myself."

He smiled. "I've no doubt about that. But I'd like to think we might learn to take care of each other in time."

Those words broke the spell. They reminded her that she did not have time. She had expected this to be a strange sort of vacation romance, but her heart was swelling and soon it would break.

He touched her temple with the tip of his finger

and traced a line from there down to her jaw and slowly found his way to her lips.

Her lips parted of their own accord.

"I told you that I love you," he said. "Those words dinnae come easily for me, except when I say them to you." He touched his lips to hers so lightly that she sought them, and her body sought his.

He lowered his hands to her waist and gently stepped back to put distance between them. "*Och*, lass, I would take you right here if there were not so many eyes upon us."

"What?"

He lifted his eyes toward the tower, where two men were stationed and watching, as was their duty.

"Oh—" Mac gasped and started to curse but caught herself. "I forgot."

The corner of his mouth turned up as he offered her his hand. In silence, they walked. The sky was a brooding blue-gray of a sort she had seen only in Scotland. "Ciarán?"

"Aye?"

"When I met you, you said we had loved one another."

"'Tis true."

"But you came back to me before I'd ever met you."

"Aye."

"But now that I've come to find you, you remember me."

"Aye."

"But how? What we shared—our falling in love—has not happened."

Ciarán stopped and stared out over the water. "I dinnae ken, except that when I returned from being with you this last time, I was caught by the Rosses, as you well know. But that was different from before. Things I once did were undone, I suppose. But still, I had loved you. I remember our falling in love as if it were a dream, but since I've returned, it's all new."

"But the first time that we fell in love—why were we parted?"

Ciarán's face showed a growing frustration.

Mac continued, "We were parted, but then you came back for me. Why?"

"I dinnae ken. I have tried to recall it. It seems as though I should remember, and yet I cannot."

"There must be a reason. Did something happen?"

His frustration turned to anger. "Do you hear what I'm saying? I cannae remember!" He took a few steps away, keeping his back to her.

Mac's brow creased. She did not understand what she had done to enrage him. "I'm sorry."

He lifted his hand dismissively but did not turn to face her. "'Tis not you. I have tried to remember, for I feel in my soul that something terrible happened that I need to prevent, but I cannae recall it." He turned, and his eyes burned with the torment of not knowing. "I fear for your safety."

"But you said yourself that things changed when you came back. So this might not happen at all."

"Perhaps not."

He looked unconvinced, so Mac went to him and took his hands in hers. "Don't worry about it."

"It's you I worry about, and I always will." His eyes softened as he leaned down and kissed her.

For someone who meant to go home and leave Ciarán behind, Mac was doing a terrible job of putting distance between them. But she wanted his kiss and his love, and the rest of him, too. She could not help but wonder what it could be like to spend her life beside Ciarán, but she stopped herself. She could not let herself think of that now—or ever, for that matter.

Ciarán's face lit as he smiled and gave her hand a light tug. "Come home with me, lass."

The word *home* stirred bittersweet feelings for Mac, but she tamped them all down and followed him back to the castle.

———

ONCE BACK IN HER ROOM, Mac closed the door

behind her and leaned against it. She breathed in and then sighed. She was happy. She wanted to laugh. The next moment misery washed over her. She was falling in love. After years of backing away when men got too close, she could not get close enough to this man. Too full of joy when she was with him, she could not think of the future; it would spoil the present. All she wanted right now was the joy of being with Ciarán, so she resolved to think only of that.

He had sent her alone to her room at the top of the stairs. He had matters to attend to but would see her at supper. He had hastened to add a promise that he would not leave her alone this evening. He would make it his mission to attend to her only. She had begged him not to, but his answer had been a mischievous smile.

A knock on the door she was still leaning upon startled her. "Come in, Janet," she said as she turned to pull the heavy door open.

"I'm afraid Janet's busy. Will I do?"

Wide-eyed, Mac stepped aside so Ciarán could enter. "What are you doing?" She laughed with the same laugh she usually used to keep things light when men got too close. But when she looked at Ciarán, he was not close enough.

He leaned on the closed door with his arms folded over his chest. "Ever since I saw you watching me earlier, there's something I've been wanting to do."

Now he was getting too close. Mac could not even force her usual light laugh. Her cheeks were hot, and her heart pounded mercilessly. "That was a mistake," she said. "I just happened upon you. I didn't know you were naked. I mean, well, I knew, of course. Anyone could see that. But I wasn't trying to…" She trailed off and then walked to the window to look outside.

"Stare?" He slowly closed in the space between them.

Mac turned to face him again. "I was startled. It just took me a moment to recover."

"How long is a moment in your century?" As he said it, he stopped inches from her, a bold look smoldering in his eyes. "For it seemed like a very long moment." The corner of his mouth twitched.

This was her chance to put a wall up between them. She'd done it so many times and in so many ways that by now she could soften the most awkward moment.

She said, "It might have seemed longer to you, but it was only a moment."

But her nonchalance faltered as Ciarán leaned close, but not close enough for his lips to touch hers. She knew exactly what he was doing. So did he. He would force her to move that one last inch. And before long, she did. Her lips touched his lightly, like a flame barely touches the wick of a candle before it flares and then constantly burns. Mac lost herself in that kiss, in his arms, and against that strong body.

Her friends used to tease her about being a nun, but she had always considered herself more along the lines of particular. She knew what she wanted in a man, and she was not going to settle for less. Ciarán was more. So was her response. Her heart and her body had moved on without her, driven by passion. She hungered for him, for each kiss, for that body she had seen coming out of the water. She wanted every part of him on her and in her with a fervor that set off every internal alarm. *Step away from this man! Save yourself!* Evidently, her inner alarm had a snooze button. But even that sounded again. With a panicky sigh, she stepped back, her palms on his chest, and took deep breaths. "It's not that I don't love you. Oh, God, what am I saying?"

"I believe you just said that you love me." Ciarán was irritatingly calm, even confident. Not only that, he was smiling.

Exasperated with herself, Mac said, "I know what I said. I just didn't mean to say it."

"But you did." He brushed a few strands of hair from her face before settling his gaze on her with sheer pleasure.

She could not look away. Nor could she deny what must have shone through her eyes. "I did, didn't I?" The next moment, she forced a smile, hoping humor would rescue her. "Don't even think about saying you told me so."

"I dinnae ken what you mean."

With a light smile, she said, "It's a saying. You told me the first time we met that I'd love you."

"Aye, and what else did I tell you?"

Mac's eyes betrayed her as she met his unwavering gaze. She knew, but she did not want to reveal how she recalled every word and inflection. She tried to shake her head as though his words had escaped her, but he took her face in both hands and forced her to meet his fierce eyes.

"Tell me," he said.

It was all happening too fast. At this rate, she would have to leave soon, before inviting more heartache, but she was not ready. "You said you would love me."

His eyes softened. "And I do, and I will."

When she lowered her eyes to avoid him, a tear slid down her cheek. That was his undoing, for he gathered her into his arms and held her as if he would protect her from all the world if he had to. "Dinnae worry yourself about it, my love."

A knock at the door startled them both. Mac's eyes opened wide as she stared at Ciarán. He whispered, "Say, 'Yes?'"

"Yes?"

"'Tis Janet. I thought you might like me to help you dress for supper."

This brought on new panic, but Ciarán, who was now growing amused, shook his head. He held her head and spoke softly into her ear. "Tell her, 'No, thank you.'"

"No, thank you, Janet. I'll be fine on my own."

Mac squirmed as he brushed his lips and warm breath on her ear, making matters worse for her, much to Ciarán's delight.

"Are you sure, miss?"

"Yes. Thank you, Janet." The pitch of Mac's voice rose and lowered as Ciarán trailed kisses down her neck, and she wriggled free from his grasp.

Having managed to fend off Ciarán's advances until Janet's footsteps were well down the stairs, Mac said, "Well, now you've done it. Now I'll have to dress myself."

"I can help—although I'd rather undress you," he said with a glint in his eyes.

Mac firmly said, "No."

He acted offended. "Do you not trust my honor?"

She answered with an unimpressed stare. However, in truth, she trusted herself even less. "Seriously, someone's bound to recall seeing us both coming up here. Won't they talk?"

"*Och*, they'll talk no matter where we are. There's only one way to cure that."

The look in his eyes made her uneasy. Before he could say what it was, she said, "Never mind. I'm sure Janet's too busy to give us much thought."

"Not since you've sent her away," he said with an admonishing look.

"Really? Isn't there anything else for her to do?"

"Oh, aye. She can sit in the kitchen and gossip. That will keep her quite busy."

"Oh, great." She escaped to the window for air, which she found herself desperately needing.

He followed and lifted her chin as he leaned down to kiss her. "Calm yourself, lassie. You ken that I love you. So do they. I doubt they'll be overly harsh." He kissed her again. She was beginning to lose herself in his kiss when he stepped back. His eyes smoldered as he said, "Now, my love, I must leave you alone." He strode to the door and opened it. He paused to look back one last time with a longing that made her too weak to bound across the room and throw herself into his arms, which would have been her first choice.

"Until supper," he said as he turned and shook his head as if, by doing so, he might rid himself of the yearning.

15

PROMISE AND DUTY

As CIARÁN LISTENED to a story that Hamish was telling, he brushed his hand against Mac's as he reached for his glass then again as he set it back down, just to prove he was ever aware of her presence. When they touched, he did not look at her, but the corner of his mouth moved just enough for Mac to know he had not touched her by accident. This alone made her heart skip a beat. At some point during the meal, perhaps after his knee gently pressed against hers, she realized she enjoyed the shared secret between them. In fact, she basked not only in the attention he gave her but also in the affection behind it. She could not get enough. Gone were the fears that people were staring. Some still did, but Mac minded it less because her trust in Ciarán was growing. So was her love, and that overshadowed all else. As she sat at the table, she took pleasure in knowing that his arm was within inches of hers and might brush against hers at any moment, which it did more than once.

God, Mac, you're a wreck. But she smiled as she thought it.

After supper, the music began, and the dancing soon followed. With no warning, Ciarán took Mac's hand and pulled her from her chair.

Mac shook her head. "No, I wouldn't begin to know how to do some of these dances."

"We're not going to dance. Come with me."

They made their way through the crowded hall to some stairs Mac had never gone up. Ciarán led the way up the narrow spiral of stairs and along a narrow passage until they reached the top and stood at the parapet. Ciarán nodded to a guard, who discreetly left them alone. Ciarán stopped at a notch in the wall that afforded a view of the moon as it lit a path over the water. "I've been coming up here since I was a boy. I think more clearly here."

Mac took in a deep breath. "I can see why. It's beautiful."

"It is," Ciarán agreed. He brushed his fingertips over her hair and then turned her shoulders so that she faced him. Gently, he slid his palms down her shoulders and arms to take hold of her hands, which he kissed. He glanced up from her hands, and a smile spread to his eyes. "I've made no secret of it. I love you."

Mac could not help but smile in response. This strong, confident man looked a little bit nervous. Beneath his thick brown hair, his brows rose, hopeful and yet unsure, causing lines to stretch across his forehead. It was too dark to see the blue hue of his eyes. She could only see how troubled they were.

"Is something the matter?" she asked.

He ran his fingers through his hair. "*Och*, lass, I'm sorry." He circled his strong arm around her shoulders and drew her to him. There he held her against him for a moment. "Nothing is wrong." After a kiss on her forehead, he put space between them but still held her shoulders. "Mac, I'm the second son. Hamish may not be the most caring older brother, but he respects me and values my presence."

"I'm sure that he does." Mac's brow creased. On a night like this, this seemed an odd choice of conversation topic.

With barely a pause, Ciarán went on. "I've a home in the castle for now, but there's a bit of land I've been told I might build upon."

"Oh, I hear you. I could never live in the same house as my sister. My God, as much as I love her, I'd kill her—if she didn't get to me first." Mac laughed, but he did not join in.

Ciarán seemed unusually pensive. "What do you think of life here?"

"I won't lie, it's different, but I'm getting used to it. Although, I have to tell you, I'd kill for a blow-dryer— and some cotton swabs! Why didn't I think to bring those? I could wax an SUV with what's building up in my ear canal."

He frowned. "I dinnae ken what you just said."

Mac started to explain but stopped herself. "Oh, never mind. I don't know what I was saying, except there's something about you that's making me nervous."

"Is there?"

"Yes. For instance, I'm pretty sure you've left a full set of prints in my shoulders."

He looked puzzled until she smiled and looked down at one shoulder, which he held with a formidable grip.

He let go instantly. "*Och*, I'm sorry." If the edge in his voice had not been clue enough, his turning to lean on the wall made it clear. Ciarán MacRae was not pleased, and she was pretty sure she was the cause.

Now he had her attention. Softly, she said, "I'm sorry, but I don't understand. Is something wrong?" She touched his arm.

He whirled around, hooked one arm around her

waist, and pulled her into a kiss that took her breath away. As her feelings careened out of control, the thought flashed through her mind that at least there was one thing they knew how to do well together.

When they finally stopped for sheer want of oxygen, Mac said, "So I guess this means you're not mad at me."

"If you mean cross, no, I'm not." He shook his head, but there was a grin in there somewhere.

Still dazed, Mac could not take her eyes from his. "Good, because I'd like to do that again." She reached up to put her arms around his neck, but he took hold of her wrists.

"No, not yet. First, you must listen to me."

Mac bristled at his commanding tone. "Yes, sir."

Her sarcasm had no effect.

"Mac, would you live here with me as my wife?" A deep sigh punctuated the question. He quietly added, "My God, will all of our talks go as poorly as this?"

The only sound for a moment was the lapping of water as it met the small island shore.

"What did you say?" Mac asked softly.

"Are you serious, lass?"

"The exact words?"

"Woman, dinnae vex me. You ken what I said. I've asked you to live here with me as my wife."

Mac slipped her hands from his but then ran her fingertips over his hands and held them. "I can't."

It was he who moved first, gently pulling his hands from her grasp and taking a step back. He nodded, as though his heart might follow, agreeing. Abruptly, he took her hand. "I'll see you to your room now."

"Wait, Ciarán. Let's talk."

"I've nothing to say."

"But I do."

"Well, you'll not say it now."

"Ciarán, please."

Without another word, he led her to her room and saw her safely inside. The oak door grated against the stone frame as he closed it. Mac sank to the floor and wept.

————————

FOR THREE DAYS, it rained. Without saying good-bye, Ciarán had gone. Mac had been given no chance to explain, not that any explanation would help. The result was the same. They could not be together.

By the third day, Mac wondered why she had not left too. But she knew the answer. She could not bring herself to leave him without seeing him one last time. She owed him that much, and she wanted that much for herself.

Mac was sleeping her troubles away in the midafternoon when she heard a large oak door close with a dull thud that filled the small corridor. Mac rushed over to Ciarán's door and knocked, doing her best to imitate Janet's knock. His weary response proved he'd accepted her ruse. She went in.

Ciarán began to say something as he turned, but he halted when he saw Mac.

"Ciarán, I'm sorry, but I needed to see you."

She could almost hear him thinking that he did not need to see her, but instead he clenched his jaw and waited for her to explain. His blue eyes clouded with pain, leaving Mac feeling she'd lost herself there.

"You can't think I don't love you," she said.

"I'd hoped that you might." He spoke with great care to keep his voice even, and he almost succeeded.

She looked around, hoping that not looking at him directly might quell the pain. It was a man's room, with tapestries on the wall; fur and thick quilts were draped over the bed, and a fire blazed in the fireplace. Mac found it bold, masculine, and perhaps a bit dark.

She had had three days to rehearse what she wanted to say, but still she struggled to get the words out. "If you'd asked me simply to marry you, I'd have found it hard to say no." She let her sad eyes settle on him.

He flashed a bitter look and then turned away—probably to maintain his control, she suspected.

She knew she had hurt him, so she tried to sound gentle. "Instead, you asked me to stay here with you." She looked up and sighed as tears made their way to the surface. "And that is something that I cannot do."

He would not look at her, so she stepped closer and laid a hand on his shoulder. This simple touch made her want more. "No matter how much I love you," she finished.

He exhaled through his nostrils, pulled away abruptly, and strode over to the window. He looked out, his back erect. "I understand. There's no need to explain any further."

Mac moved closer and reached out to him but then withdrew her arm without having touched him. "But there is." She drew close, just behind him, close enough to rest her head on his shoulder, but she resisted and looked out through the window with him.

Ciarán shifted his weight as if he might leave. Mac put both hands on his shoulders. He tensed but made no further effort to leave, as if her light touch could hold him there.

She began quietly. "When my parents died, all I had was my sister, and she had no one but me. We were lost and alone in the world, except for each other. We made a promise never to leave one another alone. And I can't break my promise to her." She brushed her hand over his shoulders and the curves of his muscles. "No matter what. And I couldn't leave without having you know how I feel. Only a love that is deep and true could hurt me like this because that's what I feel. I can't help it."

He glanced back over his shoulder and, seeing her, lost any wall of restraint he imagined he had built. He opened his mouth to say something, but he turned and kissed her instead. Mac abandoned herself to that kiss, for she knew they would part. And she knew she would never know love like this again.

The kiss ended, but Mac gripped his leine. "If I have to spend my life missing you, give me something to remember."

Ciarán's eyes clouded as he shook his head. "It will only hurt more."

"Not tonight. We won't let it."

He fixed a dark look on her, barely moving. Mac waited. She was sure he would send her away, but she clung to each second. The next moment, he scooped her up into his arms and carried her in long strides to his bed, where he lay her down and climbed onto the bed, straddling her. Leaning over, he cupped her face in his hands and said, "I cannae leave here. I've a duty to my clan, for you ken that I'm needed. But what I need is you, and I think you need me." Without waiting for a reply, he put his mouth on hers and kissed her with fervor enough for a lifetime. For one night, they would let go of promises and duties and give in to the need to be one. For as much as their bodies were driven, their souls sought it more. For without this one night, they would not be complete.

16

TOMORROW

THE NEXT MORNING, Ciarán woke Mac with a kiss. Then he rolled onto his back and lay down, his eyes closed. Mac rolled onto her side and leaned on her elbow to watch him. She had noticed his lips, soft and full, from the start. The outer edges turned up just a bit. She had studied his mouth while he stared at the fire on the night they first met. Now she traced her fingers over those lips until she gave in to desire and kissed him again. Taking her face in his hands, he bored a dark look into her eyes and then rolled over onto her. He buried his face in her neck and let out a soft groan. His lips brushed against her earlobe as he whispered, "I must go, bonnie Mac."

Mac answered by wrapping her legs around his waist.

Ciarán laughed, but not without frustration. "*Och!* Dinnae tempt me."

Mac smiled mischievously. "Why not?"

Ciarán's answering smile went as quickly as it had come as he brushed his knuckles over her cheek. "Because…" He eased himself off her and sat at the edge of the bed.

Mac sat up, clutching the covers to her chest. "Ciarán?"

"You should go back to your room before Janet comes up and finds your bed hasn't been slept in."

"Let her talk."

"No, I'll not have servants talk."

"I'm sorry. I sometimes forget how different your life is."

Mac saw the full weight of Ciarán's troubles on his face. Some she knew, but there must be more, for his brow was too creased and his eyes far too distant.

He said, "I have tried to live my life with honor for the sake of my family and, one day, my wife—whoever she may be. I'll not give anyone cause for regret."

For a moment, Mac felt as though there were no air in the room. "No, of course not." She had not considered the fact that he would one day marry—with or without her. How could she expect him to remain alone after she had gone?

He turned to her but looked away just as quickly,

having seen the look on her face. She had tried to conceal it, but it was too late. Some things could not be hidden. Where Ciarán was concerned, her emotions were far too close to the surface.

With scarcely a glance, he reached back and put his hand over hers. "I'll not love another." His voice broke as he said it.

Mac flew into his arms, and they clutched one another.

"I don't want to go," she said.

Ciarán put his fingers over her mouth. "I ken that you must go, for you've promised your sister. Our families are what our lives are built on. You cannae abandon yours any more than I could mine. But know that I'll feel your loss."

The mere thought of actually leaving him to walk through the stone chamber made her feel like she'd been struck in the chest. Every muscle contracted. Unable to even form words, she buried her face in his neck.

After kissing her forehead, Ciarán said, "I may have to marry one day—for the clan or my family. If I must, I'll not have what we've shared whispered and snickered about in servants' quarters." He pulled her away and held her face in his hands, his eyes burning with passion. "But dinnae think that I'll not long for you every day of my life with my heart and my body. For though we're not married, you're my one true love. I gave myself to you, and you gave yourself to me. And that cannae be undone in our souls."

Ciarán's words tore down every wall she had built to protect herself. But there was no help for her now. Her heart was his, and she was at his mercy.

As he stroked her hair and her back, Mac's door across the hall scraped against the stone frame. They both stiffened and stared at the closed door to the hallway as Janet called out for Mac. Ciarán rose, pulled on his leine, and made a sloppy job of putting his plaid on and belting it around his waist. Then he opened the door a crack and closed it gently behind him. Mac heard his footsteps cross over to her room. No more than a few minutes later, he returned with a grim expression.

"Well?" Mac said, looking up as she quickly tightened the last knot in her stays.

"I dinnae think she will talk. But I hate that I had to ask it of her—threaten, really."

"I'm sorry—except that I'm not, because I cannot help being with you, and I'd do it again. I'm sure you must think that I'm some sort of crumpet—"

His face unexpectedly lit up as he grinned. "No. Nor do I think you're a strumpet."

Mac could not help but laugh with him. "Whatever! I love you, okay?"

The light was now back in his eyes, and the strain was almost gone from his face. Mac studied the beauty of it. The well-formed planes and features were almost perfectly sculpted, with lines from smiling around his mouth and eyes.

Ciarán looked toward the window. "Look at the sun. 'Tis too late for you to leave today."

She said calmly, "I know." In truth, she was glad for each kiss and each touch, for each moment her body was formed to his, which she did her best at this moment to accomplish.

Ciarán scooped her up into his powerful arms and carried her back to his bed, where he set her down gently and climbed in beside her. "Tomorrow."

His longing left her able to whisper, "Tomorrow."

He rose to his knees and unbelted his plaid. With a gentle smile, Mac took her time helping him to unwrap it, enjoying each muscle and curve as she saw it and breathing in his scent and the warmth of his breath. She was desperate to memorize all of it. When the full length of his body was against hers, the touch of his skin made her feel whole. With unabashed sorrow and yearning, they made love with slow and lingering caresses in hopes of keeping tomorrow at bay.

———

TOMORROW DID NOT COME the next day or the day after. Mac could not summon the courage, and

Ciarán did not press her. After the first few days, he stopped asking. They fell into a tacit agreement to spend what time they had together with no questions asked.

The castle grew busy with a different energy among its inhabitants. Mac had sensed similar tension when working with children. There was not always a cause one could pinpoint, but it was there. And it was here in the castle as supplies were carried about and men trained with swords and flintlock rifles. Mac would round a corner, and hushed conversations would stop. Ciarán had said nothing. Although she trusted him to tell her about anything that might affect her, she was not as sure that he would tell her about things that might affect him.

In the late afternoon, Ciarán finished training with his men and met her at a spot by the loch where they had taken to meeting secretly. Mac had been for a run around the castle grounds while Ciarán trained. She was kneeling by the water drinking from her cupped hands when Ciarán walked up behind her and said, "Hello."

Mac jumped and cried out, which brought a hearty laugh from Ciarán before he took pity and pulled her into his arms. "What is it, lass?"

"What do you mean, 'What is it?' How could I not be on edge? Something's obviously going on, but no one will tell me about it. But I see the guards doubled up, and the amount of training you guys do is insane. There are men forging weapons twenty-four, seven. Do you think I don't get it?"

"Get it?" Ciarán repeated, although he had grown used to not quite understanding all that Mac said.

She explained, "You're going to war—or to some sort of battle. I'm sorry I wasn't a better history student, but I don't know what it is, and I wish you would tell me."

Ciarán opened his mouth to reply, but Mac went on. "Because if it involves you, I should know. Do you think I wouldn't care if your life was in danger? Because, just to make things clear, I do care."

Ciarán patiently watched her until she had had her say.

Evidently, she was not quite finished. "Because, if you hadn't noticed, I've stayed here way longer than I should have because—dammit—" She started to cry and was furious at herself for it. "I love you, okay? And I have to go home, and I don't want to." A sort of frustrated growl came from her throat. "I was not going to do this."

Ciarán cradled her head as she laid her cheek on his chest. Kissing her hair and her forehead, he said reassuring words that would never come true, for it would not go well. Things would not sort themselves out, and they would lose each other in a matter of days. So they abandoned words and held onto each other until their sorrows and fears had grown quiet.

Thick, gray clouds rolled in with no warning and darkened the island. Mac shivered, and Ciarán wrapped his plaid around her.

Mac sighed and asked, "What's going to happen?"

"There's to be another Jacobite rising. We've got word that Spanish ships are nearing. They'll arrive in the next few days and garrison here while we gather enough men to make sure that Prince James reclaims the throne."

"You'll go with them, of course."

"I will go, but my part will be in the Highlands, so I willnae be far."

"I can't let you go." Mac stared at her hands as she said it.

Ciarán lifted her chin. "What are you saying, lass?"

She met his gaze squarely. "You could be hurt," she whispered, "or worse."

"My lovely lass, you're just frightened. All will work out as it must. I go into each battle without hesitation, and you must do the same. Dinnae wish me farewell with fear in your heart. 'Tis bad luck, and it serves neither of us."

"I'm not fearless like you."

"I never said I was fearless. But I willnae let it rule me."

Mac nodded. "You're right. I know it. The thing is, my fear has a life of its own. And so does my love. It seems to have taken control. I've been wrestling against it with logic, but it pretty much laughs in my face." She glanced up with a sheepish grin. "Yeah, I'm now officially nuts." But even as she smiled, tears filled her eyes.

Ciarán shook his head. "Dinnae *fash yersel*."

"Too late. I've been *fashing* myself for the past several days."

"Has it helped?"

"No."

"Come, let us walk for a while." He held out his hand with a smile that disarmed her. Without telling her where they were going, he turned and began walking. Mac followed along, content not to think about anything but the feel of his hand, the mist that was settling around them, and the rhythmical sound of the water as it came to the shore.

A strong breeze blew from the water. Mac tightened her arm around Ciarán's waist and pulled the end of his plaid over her shoulder. "I don't know if I'll ever get used to this Scottish weather of yours."

Ciarán paused. He took in a breath as though he might say something, but then he stopped himself. His jaw tightened as he looked over the water.

Mac silently chided herself and then said, "I'm

sorry. I keep catching myself thinking that we have a future. It's not good to keep dreaming."

His eyes shone with forgiveness. "I do the same thing. 'Tis torture."

With sad longing, they indulged in a lingering gaze until Ciarán said, "I've grown weary of walking. I want to be with you, alone. Shall we go home?"

17

THE SPANISH FRIGATES

THEY WERE NEARLY at the castle gate when the sound of shouting guards drew their attention upward. The Spanish frigates had been sighted. By morning, a few dozen Spanish marines were garrisoned in the castle. Mac watched as Ciarán and Hamish played host to George Keith, the Earl Marischal of Scotland, and William Murray, Earl of Tullibardine, who brought with them forty-six Spanish soldiers.

Based on their conversations, Mac pieced together the key points of the plan. A fleet carrying seven thousand Spanish marines was on its way south to England. There, the thrust of their attack would take place, but first they needed to gather a thousand Highlanders to march on Inverness. This would draw the British away from their intended attack, thus laying the groundwork for their defeat.

Despite being caught up in hosting and military preparation, Ciarán found brief moments to whisk Mac into a corner and kiss her senseless. Then duty would call, and he would be gone just as quickly. When Ciarán stole glances at Mac, Hamish would bark for him to pay attention. "Did you hear me? I said they've only brought powder, but the cannons are on another ship."

"Aye, I heard you." Ciarán gave him an impatient look, but the truth was, he had caught Mac's eye and smiled and lost track of what Hamish was saying. He could not fault Hamish for his anger, for this particular fact was important and potentially disastrous for them. They could only hope that the remaining ships would arrive soon.

Mac wondered how wives managed to watch husbands make plans for what could be their demise. But she was not a wife. Perhaps if she and Ciarán were married, they might be more at peace and thus better equipped to face what lay ahead. But they did not have the strength of a marriage to bond them together whatever might come. They were two people who were in love but were destined to lose one another.

Late one night, Ciarán arrived at her door, just as he now did every night. In he swept and wasted no time in drawing her to him. She rested her head on his chest, with her palm close beside, and gave in to the rhythm of his breathing and the beat of his heart.

"I must leave in the morning," she said softly.

His arms tensed around her. "You'll be safer in your own home."

"So will you." She lifted her chin and smiled softly. "I'm a distraction."

"No, lass. Never that."

She held up her hand to silence him. "I've completely annoyed Hamish."

"*Och*, Hamish. Dinnae worry about him."

"And I've distracted you from your duties."

He lowered his hands to her hips and pulled her against him. "'Tis a diversion I welcome."

He did his best to demonstrate, but their playful kissing and touching grew fervent. Mac combed her fingers into his hair and held his head still as she quietly said, "I will always love you."

He looked at her with fiery longing. He swallowed but could not force back the emotions that gripped him.

Mac said, "Is there a chance we might ever meet again?"

"Aye, but the stone chambers have been known to fail. I dinnae ken what makes them work when they do. Perhaps it's just the right combination of light at each end. But there's no way of knowing."

"We can try."

His lips spread in a fond smile. "Aye, that we can."
His smile faded, and a clouded expression replaced it.

Now concerned, Mac said, "We will try, won't we?
Ciarán?"

He looked as though he had just had the wind
knocked out of him. "We may not remember to
try."

"What do you mean? I could never forget you!"

Ciarán shook his head in dismay. "The time can
shift when we travel. I cannae always remember."

Mac nearly stopped breathing as she stared at
him. "No."

Ciarán nodded. "Do you recall when we met the
last time?"

She answered in hushed tones. "When I met you,
you said that we'd loved one another before."

"Aye. That's the part that's been driving me mad!
All I knew was that I loved you. That was why I went
back to find you. And I did. But I cannae recall why
we parted in the first place. For when I came back this
time, getting caught by Clan Ross changed
everything. "

Mac's brow creased. "Since I met you, I've
wondered why you left me so quickly."

His forehead was lined. He looked almost angry.
"I had to." He shook his head in frustration. "*Och!* I
dinnae ken why, but I'm burning to know. It's impor-

tant." He sank down to the edge of the bed and buried his face in his hands.

Mac held his head to her chest as he had so often done for her. "Dinnae *fash yersel*, Ciarán." He looked up and returned her reassuring smile as he put his hands around her waist and caressed her.

There was no more talk in the dark hours before dawn. Morning's light would take her away soon enough. And so, with an urgent need to be close, they made love with a vehemence that spoke of their love and their hopeless desire to cling to it. Then they drifted to sleep, despite vowing that they would not waste a moment together.

———

THEY WOKE TO A THUNDEROUS BOOM, and then another. Ciarán bolted out of bed and grabbed his sword.

"What was that?" cried Mac as she gathered her clothes and began frantically dressing.

"We're under attack!"

Ciarán made quick work of donning his plaid while Mac pulled on, laced, and tied all her layers of clothing. But before she was finished, he said, "Stay here. Bolt the door." Without waiting for her response, he grabbed his sword and his pistol and bounded out the door and down the stairs.

"Well, I'm not about to just sit here and wait," Mac muttered as she finished dressing and left. As much as she wanted to think of herself as some sort of fearsome warrior princess, she was not really sure where to start. She knew nothing of fighting or battle, so she headed down the stairs to see what the other women were doing. To her surprise, they were arming themselves with flintlock rifles.

"Can you shoot a rifle?" asked the cook.

Mac shook her head to this and to each question that followed.

"Pistol? Sword? Bow and arrow?"

By the time she was finished, Mac felt like she would do them more harm than good, which was probably true.

The cook handed a rifle to Mac. "Here. May as well learn now. Janet will show you."

The women climbed the stairs to the battlements, where the men were already engaged in the fight.

"Stupid question," Mac said to Janet, "but who are we shooting at?"

She could see that Janet patiently hid her reaction. She answered respectfully, "The British. They heard of our plans and came after us here."

They spent the next few minutes learning to load a flintlock rifle and how best to aim it. Janet, trying to encourage Mac, said, "There's enough of them there that you're bound to hit something."

Mac did not find that helpful, but before she could say so, a lead ball whistled past her and landed with a thud in the battlement wall behind her. Mac fell flat to the stone floor.

Janet grabbed hold of her shoulder. "Miss Cooper?"

She reached up and patted Janet's hand. "I'm okay." Tentatively, Mac sat up, taking care that she was well-shielded by the wall. For several seconds, she pressed her back to the wall and reminded herself to breathe in and out. She felt almost removed, as though she were watching a film of herself taking part in an eighteenth-century Scottish battle reenactment. "Someone just took a shot at me."

"Aye, Miss Cooper. They'll do that and worse if they get inside the castle walls."

Mac's head was clearing, even if her stomach felt weightless. And then anger mounted until she felt closer to rage than she had ever felt in her life. Then she pivoted around, took a breath, and exhaled as she fired. She spun around again and leaned her back against the wall while she reloaded. As she did, she felt a sense of control coming back, which she had not felt since she had walked through the stone chamber.

Janet noted Mac's newfound strength with approval as she watched her reload. "That was braw. Now let us fire again."

Mac met Janet's eyes and felt proud to have her

servant's approval. Turning, she fired again. She did not linger long enough to know whether her shots were hitting their marks, but at least she was helping the cause. There were cries from the wounded on both sides of the wall as the rifles and cannonballs struck their marks. This was what she would remember, if she survived. Beneath the cracking of guns and the boom of the cannon was a layer of anguish, the sounds of which would hang in the air long after the fighting was over.

Showing no signs of stopping, the British continued to bombard the castle with cannonballs and gunpowder explosions, bringing chunks of the castle down piece by piece. The floor shook beneath them as a section of battlement beside them broke away and crumbled to the ground. Mac reflexively scuttled backward, but the wall underneath was still swaying.

"Miss Cooper." Janet tugged on Mac's arm and then yanked her away toward the stairs as the wall fell where she had just been standing.

They rushed down the narrow spiral of stairs. When they arrived on the ground floor, they found dead and injured people strewn everywhere. Cannonballs had destroyed much of the outer wall, leaving the ground littered with fallen stones and fallen men. Mac took it all in with unnatural numbness until a large hand gripped her arm.

Mac jabbed her elbow into whoever had grabbed her. "No!" Then she reeled around, kicking and pounding as hard as she could.

"Mac!" Ciarán grabbed her shoulders and struggled to hold her until she looked up and saw his face. Her arms went limp as he clutched her to him for a brief moment. He bent his knees and crouched down to look at her eye to eye. "Are you all right, lass?"

She nodded. "I'm sorry. I don't know what I was doing. I'm okay."

He nodded and grasped her hand. "Janet, will you come with us?"

"Sir, my mother's been wounded." She had already seen her but had stayed with Mac, as was her duty.

Ciarán gave Janet an approving nod. "Go to her, Janet. And thank you for keeping Miss Cooper safe."

With a smile, she thanked him and left.

"Come, lass." Ciarán led Mac back inside through a door on the opposite side of the castle.

Mac followed, too overwhelmed to ask where they were going. She had read about battles and watched them in movies, but she had never understood until now how close and how patient death was. It would wait for the dying to suffer, no matter how long it might take for life to drain from them. Without question, Mac followed Ciarán through a hidden door to a passage.

He lit a torch and guided her through a long tunnel. "It might be too late for the chamber to work, but 'tis a clear day, thank God, so we might have a chance." At the end of the tunnel was a thick wooden door. Because the door was swollen with moisture from the water surrounding the castle, Ciarán struggled to open it without making noise. When he finally succeeded, he put out the torch and eased the door open. He put a dirk in Mac's palm and wrapped her hand around it, and then he took hold of his own and slipped outside while she waited behind. Seconds later, the door opened again. He held out his hand, and she took it and followed.

"It's high tide. Can you swim?" he asked.

"Yes."

While he wrapped his kilt tightly around him and belted it in place to make swimming easier, he said, "The British will be focused on the castle, and the men who remained behind will fight."

"Remained behind?"

"Aye. We've lost. Hamish and some of the others will fight to draw attention from those who are scattering. He'll be joining us soon."

Once in the water, they swam the short distance to the other shore, where they stayed nearly submerged and watched for the best chance to run for the trees. They were almost there when Mac heard a hiss.

When it stopped, she looked down and her head swam at the sight. Blood began seeping through her clothing. She had been shot in the shoulder. Ciarán lifted and carried her into the woods until he was sure no one had followed them. There he set her down and proceeded to tear a long strip from her skirts and tie it over the wound. Blood drained from Mac's face just before she wilted and drifted out of consciousness.

Now that she was bandaged, Ciarán cradled Mac in his arms and headed toward the stone chamber. When she became conscious again, she demanded that he let her walk, which he did, but she did not last long. She was weakening and losing a lot of blood, so he picked her up again and went on. But the British were nearing the chamber.

As he carried Mac with a watchful eye on her, Ciarán said, "Tell me what to do when we get to your time. How will I find a physician to attend to you?"

Mac told him where her house was and where she hid the key. Taking breaks to gather strength just to talk, she did her best to explain how a phone worked. "Just pick it up and press the numbers nine, one, one. Tell them someone's been shot, and they'll take care of the rest."

When they arrived at the chamber, Ciarán set her on her feet and held out his arm, signaling her to go first. He followed close behind, his arm around her waist for support. Mac turned, eyes shining with love, and made her best effort to hide how much pain she was in. As Ciarán fixed his eyes on her, a loud boom echoed, and everything shook as a cannonball struck the chamber. The force pulled them apart as the chamber caved in.

18

THE RISING

THE AIR TASTED OF DUST. Ciarán wanted water so much that he fought his way back to consciousness to get it. He opened his eyes but could not move his arms or his legs. As his vision came into focus, he saw piles of stones pinning his arms, and the memory came back. Mac had gone into the chamber ahead of him before the cannonball hit. She was still there, buried alive. Ciarán started to dig himself out, freeing one arm and then another. His legs were the hardest. Pinned down as they were, he could not reach them. He twisted and did all he could, pushing and pulling one rock at a time. At a time when speed mattered, he could only make slow progress pulling and pushing at stones one by one.

"Ciarán!" One of his clansmen rushed to him and

pulled the remaining stones away. "Hamish told me to find you. We're away to—"

Ciarán cut him off. "Ivor, Mac's under here! Help me."

Three more men caught up to them and pulled at rocks, heaving them away and scooping out dirt. After an hour, they broke through.

Ciarán called out, but there was no answer. When they had dug out an opening large enough for a man, Ciarán climbed through. He told the others to keep digging to let more light in. From what he could see so far, the chamber was empty. He called Mac's name again and again until enough light shone into the cave to propel him through to the other side.

———————

HE WAS THROUGH. But the seasons had changed. He had arrived in the midst of a terrible snowstorm. Mac had told him where her house was, so he made his way slowly through snow that came up to his thighs. He could not see her house yet, but he knew it was somewhere along this road. Just then, a car drove past. It was her car. He had seen it before, and he knew what would happen. She crashed into the side of the mountain. He rushed to the car and forced open the door.

"Come, lass," he said as he pulled her from the car. "Can you stand?"

He set her on her feet, but her legs buckled. He scooped her up. Fuzzyheaded, Mac leaned on his chest. Her hand rested on his shoulder, and her fingers traced a fold of wool draped over his doublet.

"Nice kilt, Scotty. But just so you know, real Scotsmen go shirtless." She smiled and laid her head on his shoulder.

Ciarán took her back to the stone chamber and built a fire while she slept. For the rest of the night, he tried to forget what lay behind him in the past. His brother was there. He would have to go back and help him regroup. They had lost the castle, but they would meet up with others to finish the fight they had started. He would do this for Hamish, but tonight was for Mac. He had this one night to be with her, still not knowing whether she would survive her wound from the battle. While he ached to know, all he could do now was to care for her through the night as he had once before. In the morning, he would have to return to the battle. Only after the battle was over would he be free of his duty to Hamish and to his clan. Then he would return to Mac—again and again if he must, until he was sure she was safe.

THE NEXT MORNING, his heart broke to kiss her good-bye, but she had only just met him. With the same fading restraint that had kept him from breaching the distance between them all night, he held back. But, as though she saw through his gaze to his heart, she lifted her lips to meet his.

With a groan, he whispered, "It is not our time now, but I'll come back for you, Mac." He smiled, hoping it might hide the longing. "Lovely Mac, I will love you, and you will love me." He glanced at the bright sun shining into the stone chamber. "*Och*, 'tis time."

Mac opened her mouth to ask what he meant, but he stole one more kiss.

"Remember this moment. I promise you more." He turned and walked into the stone chamber, vowing to himself that he would come back for her.

"Ciarán, where are you going?"

He turned to look back, and he smiled. "I'm a traveler, lass. I cannae stay here." There was so much more to it, but it was all that she needed to know.

"I don't understand."

"You'll think me daft if I tell you, but you'll ken when I'm gone."

"No, I think you're daft now." She smiled.

Ciarán would remember that smile. He said, "I live in the past."

"Me too. That's what Cam always tells me, but—"

"Mac, listen to me." With a flinch, he pulled back. He could feel the surge through his body that that would carry him into the past. He would be leaving her soon. "'Tis too late." He held his palm up to caution her to stay back.

Ignoring his warning, Mac rushed toward him and held his hand. A shock traveled from his hand to hers, and she pulled back.

If he allowed her to touch him again, she would be pulled back in time with him, which was tempting but out of the question. He would not do that to her. She had made it clear that she did not want to leave her sister behind, and he would honor her wish. "Dinnae touch me again."

"But why?" She rubbed her wrist.

He had no right to ask it of someone who barely knew him, but he did. "Will you wait for me?"

"Yes, if you kiss me like that again." Mac's lips spread into a smile that would not be repressed.

"You're the one who kissed me." Had it been up to Ciarán, however, that kiss would have happened hours before. But he was thankful for the kiss and her smile.

Blinding light shone from both sides as he went from one end of the chamber to the other. And he was alone.

CIARÁN STOOD STARING at the back of the cave until Ivor joined him. Before he could speak, they heard a rumbling. "Ciarán!" Ivor pushed him toward the opening, and the two climbed out just as the rest of the chamber caved in, leaving a heap of rocks under a settling cloud of dust.

Coughing, Ivor yanked Ciarán to the edge of the water, where he splashed water on their faces to rinse off the dust. Other men from their clan surrounded them. Across the water, the British were putting to use their 340 barrels of gunpowder to blow up the castle and leave it in ruins.

As Ciarán stared numbly while British destroyed his home, he seemed to awaken from his reverie. "Hamish." With growing urgency, Ciarán said, "Hamish—where is he?"

But by then, Ivor was gripping Ciarán's shoulders. Their eyes met. "He would not leave the castle. He stood on the ramparts and fought until a cannonball struck the wall where he stood. It collapsed underneath him."

Ciarán stared, uncomprehending.

Ivor said, "I tried to stay with him, but he insisted I find you and tell you to go on without him."

Ciarán was quiet. "I should have been by his side fighting with him."

Ivor squeezed Ciarán's shoulder. "You had your lady love to protect."

"And I've lost her as well."

One of the other men said, "We were under attack. You did what you could."

"Aye, but it wasnae enough." Ciarán walked into the woods. One of the men started to follow, but Ivor held out his arm to stop him.

When Ciarán had gone far enough into the dark shade of the woods, he buried his head in his hands. The weight of the day's sorrows pulled him to the ground. The two people he'd loved on this earth had left him, and he was alone. He sank down and leaned back against a tree. Eyes closed, he sat there and wished that the ground would just open and take him so he would not have to feel.

Making no effort to conceal their footsteps, the handful of men he had left behind joined him. Ivor said, "We must go."

Without opening his eyes, Ciarán exhaled the breath he had been holding and shook his head.

With a steely gaze, Ivor said, "We cannae stop now. 'Tis a cause greater than us."

Ciarán looked up from an expressionless face. "I've nothing left."

"And your lady? Would she have you quit?"

"What does it matter? I've lost her."

Ivor said, "But you've not lost your clan. The men look up to you, and they need you to lead them."

Ciarán stared blankly into the woods.

Ivor's gaze did not waver. "Do it for Hamish. Finish what he started."

Ciarán's emotions sprang to life as he turned a sharp look on Ivor.

Unfazed, Ivor gave him a gentle nod.

Ciarán set his jaw and dug deep. With no more words needed, Ciarán stood and left with them. There was no talk about where they were going. The plan had been set well before the British had attacked. They set out to meet those who remained.

HEADING SOUTH, the Jacobites gathered more men. By June tenth, they were twelve hundred strong, with additional aid from 250 Spanish marines. The men from Eilean Donan had joined forces with the Earl of Seaforth. Now at Glen Shiel, Ciarán and his men were readying themselves to march for Inverness the next morning. It was late afternoon when they heard the first shots. British troops were approaching. By evening, the British were there in full force, advancing along both sides of the River Shiel. With the first battle of the 1719 rising underway and the hoped-for munitions lost somewhere at sea, the Jacobites found themselves outmatched by the advancing British. By evening, they were quickly running out of options.

19

THE AFTERMATH

MAC SAT in the garden of her sister's home holding a coffee cup with the hand that was not in a sling.

Cam took a sip of her tea. "I still don't get why you won't press charges."

"Because, first of all, they didn't catch the shooter. Second, it was an accident. So let's drop it." Mac set down her cup a little too hard.

Cam gave Mac a full three seconds of her most annoyed look. "Sorry. I didn't know you had such strong feelings about it."

"I don't. But I've already been grilled by the police. Can we drop it?" Mac did not even bother to look at her sister. Her bandaged shoulder pained her enough; she did not need Cam to add to her misery.

Cam sat forward. "Well, it just isn't right to just

randomly fire a few rounds into the woods. Who does that?"

"People," said Mac. She leaned her head back and was thankful that there had been an exit wound. Finding a lead ball from an eighteenth-century flint-lock rifle lodged in her shoulder would have been hard to explain to the doctors, not to mention the police.

With a sudden bored sigh, Mac stood up. "I need something to read." She went inside to Cam's library and found the small length of shelf that held their mother's old books on Scottish history. Settling into an oversized chair, she thumbed through the pages until she found 1719.

Standing their ground at Glen Shiel, the Jacobites fought back, but the British cut through their defenses and forced them back into the mountains. By sunset, the Jacobites were forced to retreat. By nightfall, they had scattered into the mountains and vanished. A hundred men were lost on that day, and the Jacobite rising was over.

She whispered, "But what happened to Ciarán?" Was he one of the hundred? Even if he hadn't been, he was lost to Mac now. But wasn't this what she had wanted—to leave the past where it belonged? She had told him as much—that she had to come home. She could not stay with him. She had only gone back in time to see him again, not to stay. She had always known she would return. So here she was, home according to plan. Except for the part where she fell so deeply in love that she couldn't take a breath without longing for him.

"Does it hurt that much?" Cam stood in the doorway.

Mac quickly wiped her eyes. "Yes."

"Those horse tranquilizers they gave you don't help?"

"They're not horse tr—"

"Pain pills. I know." Cam swatted the air, suppressing a laugh. She waited for the inevitable snarky retort, but it never came. "Mac? Are you all right?"

"Yes." Mac suppressed an eye roll. Even she thought she sounded defensive.

Cam sat down on the ottoman in front of Mac's chair. She scrutinized Mac for a second or two and then said, "No, you're not."

Blaming the pain meds, Mac dissolved into tears. "I've lost him."

"Lost whom?"

And Mac told her. Had her defenses not been lowered by the pain medication, she might have held back the time travel aspect in favor of something that didn't sound certifiably nuts. She could have told Cam that Ciarán was visiting from Scotland, which he had been. But she did not leave it at that.

Afterward, Cam sat for a very long time without saying a word. Then, abruptly breaking the silence, she took a quick breath and exhaled. "Well, okay then. Why don't I get you a pillow?" With that, she got up and never broached the subject again.

When the pain meds wore off, Mac decided that it was just as well if Cam thought that the story was the product of a medically induced delusion. What good would it do if Cam believed her? The end result was the same. She had lost Ciarán. And that poet who said it was better to have loved and lost could just stuff it. She had always leaned more toward the "ignorance is bliss" school of thought.

Except she loved Ciarán. Damn poets.

20

THE NEXT TRAIN

Mac walked through the glass doors of the Metropolitan Opera and past the fountain. As she made a left turn around Avery Fisher Hall on her way to the subway, she pulled out her phone to check when the next train would be leaving from Grand Central Station. She had turned her phone off for the opera, so now she waited for it to boot up before going down into the subway, where she might lose her signal. The screen lit to reveal five missed calls from her sister.

Cam answered Mac's call on the first ring. "Where have you been?"

"The opera. And how are you, Cam?"

"Very funny. I've been frantic."

"Well, I don't know why. I told you yesterday I had a matinee ticket to *Werther*."

"Oh. Well, I hope it cheered you up."

"Yeah. *Werther* does that for me. So what's up?"

"Nothing."

Mac frowned. Cam's voice sounded forced, but she could not quite tell why. Usually Cam was not that hard to read. "Are the kids okay?"

"Yes," Cam answered with her "Why would you ask that?" tone of voice.

"Preston?"

Now Cam sounded impatient and a little annoyed. "Pres is fine. When are you going to get here?"

"I don't know. It depends on when I can catch the next train. An hour? Maybe an hour and a half. I don't know. I'll call you from the train."

Since the gunshot wound, Mac had been staying with her sister. Cam thought that Mac was afraid of getting shot again, but in truth, Mac had not quite been ready to face driving day after day past the stone chamber where she had met Ciarán. But from the sound of her sister's voice now, she thought it might be time, after all, to go back to her house. Cam was sounding a little controlling.

"Are you sure you're okay?" Mac asked.

"Yes, I'm fine." Cam added, "But hurry!"

"Okay, bye."

Mac smirked at the phone and wondered if Cam had lost her way coming out of the wine cellar. Cam had developed a habit of overreacting, but this seemed a bit odd, even for her. Mac shrugged it off and took a cab to Grand Central Station, where she caught the next train to Cam's Westchester hamlet.

An hour and a half later, she pulled into the driveway. Preston and Cam met her at the door with forced smiles. Mac muttered to herself as she closed the car door, "Oh, no. They're wearing their blind date smiles."

Just to torture them, Mac took her time walking up the steps. "Whatever you're up to, I'm not in the mood."

"Wait." Cam pulled her to the side of the hallway and fluffed up Mac's hair while Preston disappeared around the corner.

"Really?" Mac lowered her chin and lifted her eyes for a death glare at Cam. "Who's in there?" She nodded toward the formal living room.

"He's not there. He's in the family room."

"Who?" Mac looked off to the side rather than make eye contact with Cam.

"Come on." Cam hooked her arm into Mac's.

"I can't." The words caught in Mac's throat. She had grown almost able to go through the motions of living, but dating was not going to happen. As Cam led her along, Mac rehearsed in her mind how she would apologize quickly and make her escape.

Across the room, Preston stood next to Mac's would-be date, chatting. They stood with their backs to her as they looked through the window. The man next to Preston was tall and athletic, in jeans and a T-shirt—just her type… that is, before her type became kilted men named Ciarán MacRae. Hearing Mac's footsteps on the wood floor, the men turned to face her.

Mac's stomach went weightless along with her head.

"What?"

Ciarán fixed bright eyes on her. "Bonnie Mac."

Mac grabbed hold of the back of a chair for support.

"Are you all right, lass?" He rushed to her and swept her into his arms while she wept. He smiled as he lifted her chin. "Dinnae *fash yersel*, lass. I've a question to ask you."

Cam appeared out of nowhere, tissue box in hand. For once, Cam's timing was perfect.

All tissues dispensed with, Mac looked up to find Ciarán grinning at her. She could not help but grin too. "Look at you." She touched her palm to his chest. "You look good in a T-shirt."

Cam said, "While we waited for you, I had time to go shopping."

Ciarán leaned close to Mac and said softly, "I dinnae think she liked the blood stains on my plaid."

"Well, you clean up well." Mac lifted her face to his, touched his clean-shaven jaw, and brushed her fingertips over his mouth just before she kissed him.

A loudly cleared throat reminded them that they were not alone. Ciarán looked up and nodded to Preston and then said to Mac, "I'm told I must do this." He knelt down on one knee and looked up at Mac, who looked back through her shimmering tears. Ciarán took her hand in his. "I ken that you cannae go back with me, but I would stay here with you if you'd have me."

"You would live here?" Mac had never imagined he would. It took her a moment to absorb the idea.

"I would, under one condition."

Based on the look on his face, the condition seemed to be a grave one.

"That you marry me," he continued. When he got no response, he asked, "Will you?"

A sniffling noise sounded behind her. Mac turned and caught Preston's eye as he handed a tissue to Cam. Mac could not suppress a crooked smile.

"Lass? Is it so hard to answer?"

"No—yes. Yes, I'll marry you!"

The relief on Ciarán's face surprised Mac. Had he actually doubted her answer?

"Yes?" Ciarán leaned closer. "Are you sure?"

A light laugh escaped her. "Should I not be? Yes, I'm sure!" Mac circled her arms around Ciarán's neck as he held her against him. They kissed until Cam and Preston gave up clearing their throats and left the room in search of champagne.

AUTHOR'S NOTE

The Stone Chambers of Putnam County, NY: I have often driven by these stone chambers and wondered about them. While there is information available, much of it is conflicting. One theory is that they were built by ancient Celts. From that theory, my imagination took flight and Highland Passage was born.

The ghost of Balnagown Castle makes a brief appearance in Highland Passage. Known as Black Andrew, he was Andrew Munro, the 16th century laird of the castle. He is said to have abused his power as laird by murdering men and raping women. A day came when the villagers had had enough. They stormed the castle and hanged him by the neck from the highest window. To this day, his ghost is said to wander the castle and harass female visitors.

The 1719 Bombardment of Eilean Donan Castle:

Highland Passage takes place during this historic event in which British troops attacked the Jacobite castle. Visitors to Eilean Donan Castle can see replicas of the powder kegs that were used to blow up Eilean Donan Castle in 1719. It was not until 1911 that Lt Colonel John Macrae-Gilstrap bought the castle and began a twenty-year restoration to the breathtakingly beautiful castle we see today.

ACKNOWLEDGMENTS

Cover by Ravven
http://www.ravven.com

THANK YOU!

Thank you, reader. With so many options, I appreciate your choosing my book to read. Your opinion matters, so please consider sharing a review to help other readers.